POSSESSING JESSIE

POSSESSING JESSIE

Nancy Springer

Holiday House / New York

Library of Congress Cataloging-in-Publication Data

Springer, Nancy.
Possessing Jessie / by Nancy Springer.—1st ed.
p. cm.
Summary: High school senior Jessie, blaming herself for her selfish, manipulative
brother Jason's death, tries to comfort her bereft mother by dressing and talking
like him, but soon his spirit is taking over her life, while Jessie's best friend
Alisha desperately tries to save her.
ISBN 978-0-8234-2259-3 (hardcover)
[1. Grief—Fiction.   2. Spirit possession—Fiction.   3. Identity—Fiction.   4. Brothers
and sisters—Fiction.   5. Mothers and daughters—Fiction.   6. Supernatural—Fiction.
7. High schools—Fiction.   8. Schools—Fiction.]   I. Title.
PZ7.S76846Pos 2010
[Fic]—dc22
2009031638

POSSESSING JESSIE

Chapter One

Jessie put on her brother's True Athlete T-shirt. He was dead. She put on his blue jeans. He had been dead for a week, and it was her fault.

His belt fit around her hips. He was a year younger, a few inches taller.

She put on his white crew socks and his Nikes. They were only half a size large. She could wear them.

Jessie went to the bathroom mirror—weird, how since the minute she had woken up, she knew just what to do. She found a pair of fingernail scissors and started to cut her long, wavy hair. The nail scissors didn't work very well, but shaggy was okay. She grabbed handfuls of hair, hacked them off, and let them fall into the sink. Around her ears and the back of her head, she cut her hair messy but short. On top she left a longer stubble. When she was sure she hadn't missed any places, she took her brother's gel and spiked the hair she had left.

She checked herself in the mirror. Ever since it happened she had not been able to face herself, but she could now. The look was right and so was the hair color, light brown. And the green-brown eyes and the short, straight nose and the freckles. People always said she and her brother looked alike.

She missed him so much. Her bigmouth bad-boy kid brother. Dead. How could Jason be dead?

She did not put on any makeup or earrings or perfume. She had not worn any of that stuff since the day he died. Not to school. Not anywhere. Not even to the funeral.

Makeup looked bad when a person cried. And Jessie cried a lot.

Not like Mom.

She had not seen her mother cry at all. Not a single tear.

But Mom would not look at her.

And Mom would not eat. Not at all.

Mom would not talk, either.

Mom had not talked to her since it happened.

Not one word.

Jessie scraped hair out of the sink with her hands and buried it deep in the bathroom trash. She wiped up what was left with toilet paper and flushed it down the john. She picked up some fallen hair from the floor. Not exactly hiding the evidence, she told herself. Just trying not to upset her mother by leaving the bathroom in a mess.

Once she'd finished cleaning up, Jessie checked herself in the mirror again, took a deep breath, and thought about what she was doing.

It's the beginning of my senior year. My last chance to have a high-school life. I should be partying, finding some cool friends, maybe even a boyfriend . . .

Yeah, that'll be the day, Jessie thought. She didn't seem to know how to act the way the popular girls did, or maybe she just didn't want to. Everybody wore black, black, black, and Jessie didn't like it. To her, black was for—

Jason's funeral. Two days ago, Saturday. She remembered only blurry parts of it, of the whole week since the accident. She felt as if someone had hit her on the head and her brain wasn't working right. She could look at a slice of bread for minutes before she could think what it was for and whether she wanted peanut butter. But one thing she knew for sure: since Jason died, everything had changed.

Forget senior year.

Jessie breathed out a long sigh, got moving, went back to her room, and pulled her cell phone and her wallet out of her purse. Her driver's license occupied a plastic pocket on the outside of the wallet, and the picture of herself caught her eye. She studied it for a moment. Smile, pretty hair. Gone now.

When Mom sees me this way, she has to look at me. Then she can kill me if she wants to.

She stowed the things deep in the pockets of Jason's jeans and headed downstairs fast and heavy-footed in the Nike cross-trainers, thumping the way her brother would have. Walking into the kitchen, she stood tall and made her shoulders wide.

Her mom was sitting at the table. Just sitting there in her bathrobe. Head hanging. Not looking at her.

"Yo, Mudder," Jessie said in a deep voice.

Mom jumped, staring, her mouth open. Then she closed her mouth and gave a soft smile. "Well, hi, Sweetie," she whispered. A tear slipped from one eye.

A real tear.

Jessie felt like her chest was filling with helium. Huge relief. She went over and hugged her mom. Thank God. This crazy urge, pretending to be her brother, was okay. Mom had not only looked at her, she was talking to her again!

"What would you like for breakfast?" Mom asked.

Jessie shook her head. She usually got her own breakfast

cereal. It was nice of Mom to offer to make her something. But these days she had to force herself to eat. Especially in the morning, food felt like smashed metal in her stomach.

"Aren't you hungry?" Mom asked, looking so surprised Jessie didn't know what to say. She just shook her head again.

"Well, don't forget your lunch money," Mom said.

"Yeah, yeah," Jessie said the way Jason used to. "See ya, Mud." With a bad-boy strut she walked out the door, headed for school.

Chapter Two

Once she reached the car, she dropped her pose. Shoulders sagging, she got in and fastened her seat belt. She checked the controls to remind herself where they were before she started the car. The rental provided by the insurance company seemed nice, even smelled new. But Jessie didn't care much about cars.

It was no problem that she was taking the car and leaving Mom without one. Mom hardly ever went anywhere since she'd gone on disability. Her bad back forced her to lie down half the time. Most days she didn't even bother to get dressed, just went around in a flowered cotton bathrobe and pink vinyl slippers. Only once in a while she'd put on clothes to make a supply run to Wal-Mart, usually on Saturday so Jessie or Jason could carry the groceries and stuff for her.

Make that just Jessie from now on.

Jason was gone.

The sunny September day went dark. Jessie ached as if she had just this moment learned that Jason was dead. Over and over again this had happened. He kept sneaking up on her.

She had to go to school to keep her grades up so she could get a college scholarship. Jessie wanted to be something—she wasn't sure what yet, but something important, like a scientist to stop global warming or a doctor to find a cure for cancer. She hardly ever missed school. She had even gone to school last week, missing only one day, the day after Jason was killed.

But today, driving even more carefully than usual in the strange loaner car, she thought about actually skipping, because how was she supposed to face school dressed up as Jason? It had been an impulse that had come to her just as she woke up, and she hadn't planned beyond it. Like a miracle it had gotten her mother to talk to her, but now what?

For a person who doesn't like to be stared at, Jessie thought, *I've fixed myself good.*

She pulled into the high-school parking lot anyway, got out of the car, and tried to make herself small, head and shoulders curled over, as she headed for the main door.

Some girl screamed.

Jessie didn't look to see who.

Other kids screamed, too. Not all of them girls.

Jessie didn't look up. Kept on walking with an awful numbness, that same numbness she'd felt since Jason died.

Walking into a hubbub of voices. "What the hell is *that*?" "That is so wrong!" "Is that his sister?" "For a minute there, I really thought it was Jason." "That's sick!" "What's her name? I forget." "She scared me!" "That's cold, making fun of Jason. That's harsh." "He was a great guy." "Jennifer, Julie, something like that." "I thought I was seeing a ghost." "What's she think she's doing?" "She's got to be crazy." "What's she trying to prove?"

Jessie edged her way through the crowd. Head down, she walked on until she met an obstacle she couldn't bypass: business shoes, pressed slacks.

A teacher.

"Jessie Ressler!" the man barked at her. "Jessica!"

She looked up into the eyes of her brother's wrestling coach, who also taught American history.

He softened his tone slightly. "Jessie, I'm sure there is an explanation for this."

If there was, Jessie didn't know, except—the way it had helped Mom, was that the reason?

"Jessie?"

Feeling very tired, she let her eyes slip away from his.

He turned stern again. "Jessica, I know you loved your brother very much."

He had no idea how much. Like a lot of other people, she had practically worshipped Jason. The whole school cheering for Jason, handsome Jason grinning after winning yet another wrestling trophy, his glance finding her in the stands so he could give her a wink . . . Jessie bit her lip to keep from crying. She had adored him.

"But if this is your way of honoring your brother's memory, I must say it's in very bad taste."

Dully Jessie wondered whether she was in trouble. She'd never been in any kind of trouble in school. But compared to Jason dying, it no longer seemed to matter much.

"May I go?" she asked almost in a whisper. "I have to get to class."

"I suppose. . . . I can't think of any rule . . ." Grim-faced, Coach stood aside and let her pass.

Some kids came up to her in homeroom and asked her "Why?" But she had no answer, no response, because something, maybe the angry voices and shouting, had started the tape, a sort of video in her mind, making her live through the accident again and again. It turned itself on whenever it wanted, and she could not turn it off. Vaguely she was aware of kids calling her crazy to her face, psycho, wacko. A few of them were the same kids who had texted her after the accident: **2 bad sory, i pray 4 U, so sad, hugs hugs hugs.** But now they acted like they hated her.

As if from a distance, like she was watching through binoculars, she saw one exception—Alisha, her best friend. Alisha stepped up to defend her. With her hands on her hips, Alisha growled, "Hey, Jessie, are these jerks bothering you? If you want, I'll throw them out the window." And Alisha might actually do it. She was a big girl, a tough girl. Nobody messed with Alisha.

Jessie managed to smile and say, "Thanks, Alisha, it's okay. I'm fine." But she was not fine. She was sweating ice as the tape kept playing and the memories took over.

Chapter Three

"I wish Dad were here," Jessie had muttered as she got into the car with Jason, and that had started the same old argument.

Jason always got testosterone-prone when he was driving anyway. "Dad had a right to walk out. I mean, any man would get tired of Mom and her stupid backache."

"No, he didn't." Jessie understood how her mother felt: betrayed. Jessie felt the same way; how could her father do that to her? Just *leave* her? Like she was worth nothing? Like throwing away a paper cup? "If he and Mom had problems, he should have tried to fix them."

"Maybe he did. How would we know?"

"We know they didn't go for counseling—"

"Like Dad would go to a shrink? Give me a break. Face it, Sis, Mom wasn't giving him what a guy wants."

Ow. TMI. But Jessie pushed the thought aside and talked right past it, getting to the point she was trying to make. "But he walked out on *her*, supposedly. He didn't walk out on you and me. Why doesn't he call us once in a while?"

"Yeah, well, good question." Although Jason tried to keep his studly tone, his voice lowered. "I don't know the answer, Sis."

Silence, except for the rumble of the red car.

I thought Dad loved me.... Jessie bit her lip. Sitting in the Mustang's passenger seat, watching Jason lean too far back and hold the steering wheel the wrong way, she wished more than ever, although she didn't say it again, that her father were here to teach Jason how to pass his road test. Jason might have paid *some* attention to Dad. Not that anybody had to teach Jason how to drive. He'd been driving illegally since he was, what, thirteen? But at suppertime, Mom had said Jessie had to coach him on the rules and things the examiner would be looking for. Mom insisted they go out now, even though there wasn't much daylight left, since Jason was home for a change.

So Jason was supposed to listen to Jessie, and as they drove through town, she tried again. "Look, Jason, pull over. You have to move the seat forward, straighten it up, and steer with both hands."

"You just want me to drive like a *girl*."

Jessie felt a dull anger she didn't bother mentioning, she was so used to it. All she said was, "Just pull over."

He did, and he moved the seat up as she'd told him, then sent the red Mustang recklessly darting out into traffic again.

"Wait! Pull over." Jessie's voice was rising, even though she'd sworn to herself that she'd be cool. "You didn't fasten your seat belt."

"It won't reach when the seat's too far front like this."

"Of course it will. You *adjust* it."

"*You* adjust your attitude. Don't try to boss me around."

Jessie kept her voice calm and reasonable. "I'm supposed to be teaching you things. Such as, slow down. The speed limit here is thirty-five, and you're doing fifty."

"You sound like Mom. Lighten up, Sis, or you're gonna be a lost cause just like her." Jason pressed on the accelerator, pushing the speed up to sixty. They were almost at the edge of town, speed limit fifty-five, so it didn't really matter, but Jessie felt her usually quiet anger begin to sizzle. Lost cause? How could he say that? Mom let him do whatever he wanted, absolutely whatever. She made special snack mix and served it to him as he watched TV. Doing the laundry, Mom bleached his athletic socks snowy white. She bought him clothes and clothes, and so many different kinds of shoes—Converse, New Balance, Adidas, all the brand names—he had more stuff to wear than Jessie did. Mom's sun rose and set on Jason. He was her world.

"Jason, slow down," Jessie ordered sharply as the road narrowed.

"For gosh sake, Sis, cool it!" he said, pushing the Mustang up to sixty-five on the hilly, curving country road. "Come on, relax." He smiled, and his tone changed, eager, teasing yet serious. "I'm going to show you how to live a little."

Jessie didn't feel like living a little. She just felt scared. She would have begged him to slow down, but her fear flipped into anger. He was supposed to be doing what she said, damn it!

"If you're not going to listen," she snapped at him, "then turn around and we'll go home. It's getting dark."

"Good! Going fast is even cooler in the dark." Jason switched the headlights on, high beam, but showed no signs of slowing down.

"Look, I'm not doing your homework for you anymore unless you stop this car and turn around."

"Whoa! Now you're threatening me." He sounded amused as he drifted the Mustang through a curve, tires squealing, tree trunks flashing dizzying white in the headlights. "You really need to learn to have some fun, Sis. Tell you what. We're going to see how fast we can take Dead End Bend."

11

He was talking about the hairpin turn in the next dark road to the left, which plunged down a steep hill. At the bottom, two narrow "cow-path" roads had once crossed at a sharp angle. When the county had put the reservoir in, they had dead-ended both roads right at the intersection, so that they became one road doubled back beside the woods near the edge of the water, a small road seldom used by anybody except the few people who lived down that way.

And by boys trying to set speed records. Bright yellow barriers with black arrows had been knocked down and smashed so many times that the county no longer bothered to replace them. And barriers weren't the only things that had gotten smashed. Cars, totaled. Kids, hurt. One boy had been paralyzed, was going to spend his life in a wheelchair.

Jessie's reaction to the Dead End Bend idea was instant and panicky. "Jason, no! Don't be stupid!" Just as instantly, she knew she had made a mistake, that she should try to sweet-talk Jason, not shout at him, but she couldn't help it. She was terrified, and angrier than she'd ever been in her life. He was not respecting her. "Jason, slow down!"

He sped up, screeching around the left turn toward Dead End Bend. "This Mustang isn't bad, but a Z-car would be awesome. I bet it would do sixty-five. The fastest I've been able to drift Dead End Bend in this car is fifty."

"Jason, stop acting like an idiot! Do you want to get us both killed?"

"If I can get it up to sixty, I'll beat the record. You're my witness."

"Jason, no! Please!" Damn, he had her so scared, she was pleading with him after all.

Jason grinned. "Don't be such a wuss, Jess. You'll thank me afterward."

"No, I won't. Stop the car *now*. Please!"

"Just hang on." Night flashed past as they whizzed down the hill at sixty-five, seventy—

Left-handed, Jessie reached over and snatched the keys out of the ignition.

"Hey! What the—"

With the engine off and the power steering gone, Jason hit the brakes hard as he swore at her, grabbing for the keys. She clutched them in her hand, and his hand closed around hers so fiercely she cried out. "Jason, you're hurting me!"

"Good! I'll hurt you more if you don't give those keys back!" As the car slowed to a stop, he grabbed her forearm with his other hand, wrenching it until she started crying, until she had to let go of the keys. They dropped to the floor. He searched for them, grabbed them. But not before she had unbuckled her seat belt, opened her door, and stumbled out of the car. As he was putting the keys back into the ignition she slammed the door.

"Hey!" Revving the Mustang, Jason popped his door and shouted at her over the roof, "What the hell do you think you're doing?"

Sobbing almost too hard to speak, Jessie yelled back, "Go kill yourself and see if I care!"

"Are you crazy? Get back in here."

It was kind of crazy, because she was miles from anywhere. Still, she told him, "No."

"I said get in!"

"Go to hell."

"God damn it, Sis, get in this car."

"No." Jessie started to walk away along the dark, grassy edge of the road.

Jason threw the Mustang into reverse and cut her off, still swearing at her. "Dumb-ass, I can't just leave you out here. Get in the damn car!"

"No."

He stared at her. "Jessie, what's with you?" he asked almost as if he were the one pleading now. "You PMSing or something? I've never seen you like this."

Because she had never before felt so helpless, so desperate for control. "You get out and give me the keys." Since he had lowered his voice, she lowered hers. "I'll drive us home."

"No way." He grinned at her, friendly again. "I came out here to set the world's record going around Dead End Bend, and I'm gonna do it."

"Jason, no!" She wasn't crying anymore. She felt too dry with terror to cry.

"Oh, for God's sake, Jessie, don't get your panties in a bunch." Jason swung back into the car. "You don't have to come with me if you don't want to. Just stay where you are."

"*Jason!*"

"Stay put. I'll be back in a minute."

"Don't go!"

"Chill out, Jessie! I'll come *back* for you. I promise."

So as he sped off, Jessie stood at the side of the dark road, hearing the roar of his motor become more and more distant, trying to tell herself it would be all right; he was a good driver, even driving fast; he would be back—

Then she had heard the scream, scream, screaming of the tires, and the sickening, shattering sound of the crash.

*　*　*

But the tape in her head wouldn't rest there. It kept playing. Blurry, out of sequence, sometimes soundless, sometimes migraine-loud, but never stopping. The police and ambulance sirens shrieking, the lurid lights. But before that must have been the blackness and running, running down the hill in the dark toward Dead End Bend, telling herself her brother was all right, he had to be all right, they would take him to the hospital and make him better. Running, running so hard she could hardly breathe, but still the tears flowed. She had left her cell phone in her purse in the car, and how could she have been so stupid? She had to get to the cell phone and call 911 so Jason would live— Jason had to live.

The red Mustang had crossed ten feet of gravel shoulder and another six feet of grass to climb the biggest oak tree. Like a rumpled, mutant circus pony, it stood on its hind wheels, headlights shining into the sky, dashboard lights on and dashboard alarms peeping like little frogs. Jessie found Jason not in the car but under it, his arm sprawled on the mossy ground as if he were sleeping, the strong tendons of his fingers and perfect bend of his wrist, so beautiful, like a sculpture by Michelangelo.

They said she found her purse hanging from a limb of the tree, but she remembered only holding the cell phone in her hand and pressing the 9, the 1, and the 1. The police must have taken her away before the firemen lifted the car off Jason. She remembered riding in the back of the police car, and it felt right: she should go to jail; it was all her fault, telling Jason to go get killed. She remembered waiting in a room at the hospital, but it was like black-and-white TV, no colors, and more policemen bringing her mother in and Jessie stood up but her mother

15

looked right through her as if she weren't there. At first there was no sound. Then someone turned the sound on. Jessie heard herself sobbing. She heard her mother saying very calmly and firmly, "No. There's been a mistake. No, my son is fine. He's just gone away for a little while. He'll be back."

Days following, still black and white. Mom saying the same thing as she signed papers, the same thing to the undertaker. To Jessie she said nothing, sitting but not looking, not listening, as Jessie tried to tell her what had happened. Mom was just going through denial, the pastor from church told Jessie. The first of the five stages of grief: denial, anger, bargaining, depression, acceptance. Jessie herself seemed to have skipped straight to depression. . . . Stripping off her nail polish, scrubbing away every speck of color as if it were a sin, then clipping the finger-nails short. And crying, crying all the time.

The kids from school stopped by to take Jessie with them when they placed the white wooden cross in front of the oak tree. They talked of Jason, memories of Jason, the time he had gotten a girl he met at an out-of-town dance to autograph her bra for him to keep, the time he had stretched clear plastic over the locker-room urinals, the time he had gotten all his friends to pad the ballot box so Jessie's poem won the contest, the time he had made a bet with Coach and lost and had to wear a ribbon in his hair. And then he had somehow swiped a pair of Coach's big baggy plaid boxer shorts and run them up the flagpole to get even.

They laughed and cried. They put pictures of Jason on the oak, and the tree was already so terribly wounded by the car that Jessie could hardly bear the blows, *bang, bang, bang* as they hammered the nails in. She knew the tree would die, too. Some boys nailed up a wrestling-team sweatshirt, while the girls piled angel dolls, teddy bears, baseballs, stuffed rubber-faced monsters, flowers and letters, all sorts of gifts for a ghost around the cross that stood near the twisted roots of the tree.

Jessie had nothing to leave at the shrine. Her offerings were in her head. Several times at the hospital and the morgue and the funeral home she tried to see Jason's body. People wouldn't let her without her mother's permission. Mother wasn't talking. The autopsy was private. The casket was closed. Jessie never did get to see her dead brother, say good-bye. She wept on Alisha's shoulder amid flowers that had no colors and no fragrance.

Mom did not shed a tear.

Dad was not there. How could her father, her dead brother's father, not be there?

How could Mom not cry, not cook, not eat, not sleep, not speak? How could she just sit as if she were waiting for someone?

Colors and fragrances came back. How could they do that?

How could Jessie get up two days after the accident and go back to school? How could days go on? How could school go on?

But that was last week, Jessie told herself, determined to silence the replay in her mind. That was last week. Things were different now, because she couldn't stand it, wasn't going to stand it anymore, and she was going to make things different. She had already started to make things different.

Chapter Four

At lunch, Alisha saw Jessie at a table by herself. Okay, Jessie wasn't one of the popular crowd, but she was nice, and she normally ate with some of the B-list girls plus maybe some debate-team nerds or computer geeks. But now this thing, Jessie dressing up like her dead brother, had everybody freaked.

Including Alisha, some. But too bad. *Get over it*, she told herself as she took her tray and went to sit with Jessie.

She liked Jessie better than just about anybody she'd ever met. Jessie had a rare kind of goodness: Jessie did not care whether a kid was a prep, a jock, a punk, a goth, or a scrub. She had the brains of a prep, but she didn't wear preppy clothes, just okay clothes from Wal-Mart or somewhere. She didn't belong to any of the cliques. She didn't fit in or not fit in; she was just Jessie. She didn't care whether anybody was Jewish or Creationist or Catholic or pagan or whatever, or whether they were gay or bi or straight. She just didn't think that way. Alisha knew that when Jessie looked at her she never once thought "Black." They were just Alisha and Jessie together.

Alisha had been Jessie's best friend for long enough to know that Jessie might be too good for her *own* good. Too good, for instance, to realize what a selfish, manipulative—making her cover for him when he ditched school, sweet-talking her into doing

18

his science projects, persuading *her* to pay for getting *his* hair done—what an ego-on-smelly-feet toe fungus her brother was.

Or used to be. Jason was dead. Which would not have bothered Alisha a bit, if it wasn't for Jessie, heartbroken. Taking it so hard.

And now, so weird.

"Hey, girlfriend," Alisha said as she sat down. "That's one hell of a hairdo."

Jessie seemed out of focus at first. It took her a moment to look up and try to smile. Alisha saw tears in her eyes and knew she had to be careful. Crying at the funeral was all right, but Jessie would hate it if all the kids here at school saw her bawling.

So Alisha started to eat, complaining, "They cut this stuff into bricks and they call it spaghetti?"

Jessie smiled. "It's no worse than some of the casseroles the neighbors have been bringing." Her soft voice sounded tired.

"You're not eating your lunch. Have you been eating at all?"

Jessie didn't answer. She had that out-of-focus look again, and it was as if she hadn't heard.

"Jessie?"

"Um." Jessie managed to tune in. "Sorry. Accident keeps going through my head like a bad movie."

"Ow. That must be hard."

"It has to go away sooner or later. What did you ask me?"

"Whether you've been eating."

"A little. Alisha, I'm really getting worried about my mom. She's not eating at all. Not one bite."

Alisha checked Jessie's eyes. No tears, just a wide, dry desperation.

"And I don't think she's sleeping," Jessie went on, "and I don't think she's cried *yet*. At least not that I can tell."

Weird. During the divorce, Mrs. Ressler had cried for months.

"What does she do, then?"

"Just sits, and I get the feeling she's waiting."

"For what?"

"I can't imagine! Maybe she's lost her mind!"

Alisha just smiled without remarking that some kids were saying the same thing about Jessie. "She's had an awful shock, that's all." Jessie's mother was nice, in Alisha's experience, and baked awesome frosted brownies, but Mrs. Ressler didn't seem real strong, what with her back problems and nerves and everything. "She should go to the doctor. Get some pills."

"She won't. Since the funeral, she's not talking to anybody."

"Not even to you?"

"No. Well, not until this morning, when I put this getup on."

So that's what this is about, Alisha thought with an old anger she kept quiet because it was futile. *Jessie, the smartest kid in class, yet always in her brother's shadow. Jessie trying for her mother's attention.*

"Jessie," Alisha said gently, "that's kind of sick. I mean, just because she's taking it hard doesn't mean you have to—"

"She won't look at me!" Jessie interrupted. "She won't let me touch her or hug her. If I try to talk to her, she won't . . ." Jessie's voice started to break up, and tears pooled in her eyes.

"Okay," Alisha said softly. She reached over and laid her hand on her friend's twisting fist. "Okay, whatever, Jessie. Whatever you've got to do."

Chapter Five

After school, Jessie did not feel like working on the yearbook or hanging around to listen in on debate club or see what was going on backstage, whether there was scenery being set up or kids making props. She didn't want to talk with anybody. The text messages on her phone now said things like **pervert, u r so rong, ur sick, stop rite now, sicko.** Maybe she would not look at the phone anymore. She drove home, very carefully in the loaner car, parked on the street—there was no driveway, no garage—and walked up the short sidewalk into the little cream-colored house crowded among similar vinyl-sided houses, beige, powder blue, eggshell white. For the first time, Jessie didn't want to live here, wanted to move somewhere else.

As she closed the door, Mom's voice called from upstairs, "Is that you, Sweetie?"

"No, it's me," Jessie called back.

Only silence answered her.

The cold truth froze Jessie where she stood. Her response had been automatic, not conscious, never conscious until now: She was not "Sweetie" and never had been "Sweetie." She was Jessie or, if her mother was angry with her, Jessica.

Jason was "Sweetie."

This morning Mom had called her "Sweetie."

And God damn everything, Mom was going to call her

"Sweetie" again. Pressing her lips together to stay strong, Jessie slipped back outside, then came in again, stomping this time instead of walking quietly, and making sure she slammed the door behind her.

"Sweetie?" Mom's voice floated down, anxious, from upstairs. "Is that you?"

"Yo, Mud." In a deep voice like Jason's.

"Oh, thank goodness." House slippers pattered as Mom came running downstairs. "Did you have a good day? What would you like for supper?"

"Whatever."

Mom made chicken with cheese sauce, Jason's favorite. Jessie didn't like it, but she didn't say anything. She just ate it. Her mom was smiling. Her mom was *eating*. Her mom was talking to her. "How was school?"

Jessie grunted just like Jason.

"I thought you had wrestling practice today. Did you skip? How come?"

Mom wanted her to go to wrestling practice? Jessie felt a twinge of panic, because Mom seemed to be taking the game a bit too far. Quickly, in her own voice, Jessie said, "I got an A on a calc quiz." Jason took algebra, not calculus, and Jason never got an A.

Mom stopped smiling. Or talking. Or eating. Without a word Mom got up and scraped the food that was left on her plate into the garbage disposal. Without looking at Jessie, Mom left the kitchen, trudged upstairs to her bedroom, and closed the door. After a moment Jessie could hear the sound, muffled by pillows, of her mother weeping.

Mom hadn't wept before, at least, not to Jessie's knowledge. Maybe it was a good sign. But it sure didn't feel good, listening. Jessie felt lower than roadkill. She'd made her mother cry.

After what seemed like a long time, the sound of Mom's crying stopped, but Mom did not come out of her bedroom. It got late. Jessie didn't know whether Mom was sleeping or not, whether it would be all right to tell her good night.

She tried not to think it, but she knew: Mom wouldn't answer unless she acted like Jason.

Finally, Jessie went to bed without saying anything. But she couldn't sleep. She piled all of her stuffed animals into the bed with her, hugging her favorite, the fat yellow armadillo, as she pulled the pink plaid comforter up around her neck—but her eyes wouldn't close. She stared at the shadows on her ceiling, feeling like there was a stone the size of her clenched fists lying inside her chest.

The first time she looked at her clock, it said midnight. About the tenth time she looked, it said half past one.

"Damn everything!" Jessie kicked and punched, sending her comforter and stuffed animals flying. She lunged out of bed, threw on Jason's clothes because they were handy, picked up his Nikes, and in sock feet she sneaked out of the house. She sat on the front steps to put the shoes on.

Under a cloudy moon she walked the mile to the cemetery. It was no creepier than any other lonely place at night. Daring each other to walk into dark graveyards was a game kids played to get scared when they didn't have anything better to do. Stupid. Jessie had something better to do.

She passed through the gate and heard it creak on its hinges. She heard a whispering, rustling sound like leaves in the breeze, but there was no breeze, and there were no trees.

She didn't care.

Somebody had taken the wilted flowers off Jason's grave. It looked raw and swollen, like a hurt place in the earth. Jessie sat on the red dirt and cried.

"I—can't—stand—it," she said, sobbing. She pounded the dirt with her hands, hitting Jason. But then she made herself stop, because it wasn't his fault that she felt the way she did.

It wasn't his fault that she couldn't forget him and the way he used to tease her by hiding her homework. The way he had raced her for the bathroom in the morning. The time he had dared her to sneak into an R-rated movie. The time he had talked Mom into letting her go to a pizza party when she was supposed to be grounded.

It wasn't supposed to happen. It was an accident. It wasn't his fault that he was so fun and bad and now he was dead. . . .

Or was he?

That moment, like a mist rising up from his grave, something embraced her like a soft blanket. Something made her feel not exactly good, but calmer. It made her feel like he was there.

"Jason," she whispered.

Chill out, Sis, for God's sake.

"I can't. Mom is—Mom's a mess. She adored you. She worshipped you."

So what else is new?

"She never loved me that way."

Yeah, yeah.

"What am I supposed to do?"

You're doing okay. Just relax.

And in that moment she *could* relax. It was wonderful to be able to relax. She lay down on the soft grass, the soft grave, and when she left the cemetery about three in the morning, she felt comforted, as if she'd had a good conversation with a friend.

When she got home, instead of going to her own room, she went to Jason's. His sports posters leered down from the walls. His bed, hard and narrow under its army blanket, faced her like a monument, its surface smoothed faultlessly as usual by Mom that last morning of his life. Jessie yanked back the covers and lay down between the camouflage-patterned sheets she had always considered so ugly. Now it didn't matter what they looked like; a faint scent of Jason still clung to them. With her head on Jason's flat pillow, Jessie eased instantly into sleep.

The next morning, late, when she finally woke up, she put on some more of Jason's clothes. His 250 Club T-shirt, meaning he could bench-press that much weight. His blue plaid long shorts, the latest style. His Converse slip-ons, no socks, no shoelaces.

Her legs needed to be shaved, but so what? She didn't wear a bra, but again, so what? Her breasts weren't very big. To heck with bras. She used Jason's deodorant because she was in his room and it was handy. She grabbed Jason's cell phone; same reason.

She heard Mom moving around downstairs in the kitchen. She took a deep breath, knowing what she had to do. "Yo, Mud," she called.

"Good morning, Sweetie! I thought you were going to sleep all day. You're late for school. Come on down. I made Belgian waffles."

Careful to swagger, Jessie thumped downstairs for breakfast.

It seemed the most natural thing in the world to find Mom happy and smiling again.

Walking into school, tardy, she encountered a bunch of kids changing classes, but she didn't fold her shoulders or duck her head. The feeling she had experienced at Jason's grave, a sense of his presence, was still with her, encouraging her. She walked the way Jason would, as if she owned the place.

A teacher scowled at her. "You're late, Miss Ressler. Report to the office."

Jessie had hardly ever been late before, but she just shrugged. It wouldn't have bothered Jason, and it didn't bother her.

The teacher, a yappy-dog sort of woman, snapped, "Also, you are most inappropriately dressed."

Jessie grinned. "Yeah, yeah."

Chapter Six

Alisha's grandmother from Haiti talked about ghosts and spirits as if they were not only real but commonplace, like cats and dogs. Alisha did not believe a word of it, yet she felt her spine chill and the small hairs on the nape of her neck stand up when she saw Jessie stride into school. There was something—

Stop it, Alisha ordered herself. The only real change was that Jessie had her head up and was walking tall, like Jason. Acting like Jason, not just dressing like him. That was all. Well, and she wasn't wearing a bra, but she didn't really need a bra, so no big deal.

Yet Alisha felt something like a cold, icy, arctic rat crawl into her belly and start gnawing. At lunchtime, when she saw Jessie sitting at a table by herself, she couldn't blame anybody for staying away from her. Approaching Jessie was like walking up to a ghost. Nobody wanted to go near her.

Neither did Alisha. But somebody had to do something.

She took a firm grip on her tray—mystery meat, ick—and marched herself over to sit across the table from Jessie.

Her friend, actually eating the rather disgusting lunch, ignored her.

Pointedly Alisha said, "Hel-LO." Jessie glanced up, and Alisha looked her in the face.

Jessie stared back stony-eyed, no smile, even though she was close enough so that Alisha could smell her, and she definitely did not smell like any of Jessie's favorite perfumes from Victoria's Secret. Instead, she smelled like Axe.

"Jessie," Alisha blurted with more force than she had intended, "you're sick."

"Yeah, yeah."

"Stop it, Jessie! Talk like yourself."

Jessie put down her fork. Her face softened, and her posture relaxed. "What self is that?" she asked in her normal quiet voice. "I don't have a self."

Alisha felt so relieved, she didn't really hear what Jessie was saying. She just knew that her friend was still in there, under the spiked hair, behind the 250 Club T-shirt, and beneath the Axe.

Jessie added, "Before I started dressing up like this, I was nothing. Nobody knew who I was."

Uh-oh.

Quietly and carefully Alisha said, "That's not true. I knew who you were. Plenty of people knew who you were. Just about the smartest person in the school, that's who you were, probably going to be valedictorian, and you studied hard and stayed out of trouble and you wanted a real future—" Alisha stopped, shocked at herself for saying it all wrong, in the past tense.

"Yeah, yeah," Jessie murmured.

"Don't disrespect yourself!" Alisha tried to keep her voice down but got loud anyway. "You still *are* smart and you still *are* going to be somebody and you still *are* my best friend."

Jessie smiled, but tears shimmered in her eyes.

Alisha lowered her voice. "You are *so* a special person."

"Yeah, well, tell that to my mother." Jessie's misty glance shifted downward to the left. "She looks right through me."

"Your *mother*?" Alisha leaned forward. "Why?"

"I don't know!"

"Have you asked her?"

"She won't tell me. I told you before, she doesn't talk to me." Jessie looked back up at Alisha, her eyes wincing with pain. "She blames me, I guess."

"*Blames* you? What on earth for?"

"Because I should have died with Jason."

Alisha felt her gut lurch. "Now *that* makes a lot of sense. That would make your mother feel *so* much better."

"I'm not sure it wouldn't!"

Alisha asked softly, "Jessie, is the bad movie still running in your mind?"

"Huh?"

"You said the accident kept replaying in your head." And Alicia thought the trauma might have her confused.

Jessie stared back at her, blank, then bemused. "Nuh-uh. Not at all today. I guess it's gone."

"Good!" Alisha felt hope for her friend. "Then would you please just tell me what's going on? What happened? Why would your mother blame you?"

Jessie sighed, then said in a quiet, dead tone, "I was supposed to be teaching Jason how to pass his road test. We had a fight because he wanted to drift Dead End Bend, and—and I slammed out of the car. I told him to go get killed and see if I cared."

Alisha felt the pain behind Jessie's soft words so sharply that she couldn't speak.

Jessie said, "Then he went and did it."

Alisha found her voice. "Jessie, it's not—"

"I also told him to go to hell."

"Not your fault! Words don't make things happen."

"I hope not. I hope there isn't a hell or he's not in it."

"There isn't, and he's not, and you're not to blame."

"Yes, I am. I shouldn't have got mad at him. I should have stayed with him."

"And get yourself killed, too?"

"I should have tried to, you know, like, beg and cry, and tell him I was scared instead of yelling at him and ditching."

"I think you had every right to ditch. Did you tell your mother how stupid he was acting?"

"No. I mean, I wanted to, I tried to, but she just—looks—straight through me." Jessie started to choke up.

Alisha sat back in her chair, giving Jessie a couple of minutes to get it together, but also thinking hard.

"So if your mother doesn't want to listen," Alisha said when she thought it was safe, "and she doesn't know what happened, why would she blame you?"

Jessie just shook her head. "I was older. In charge. I wasn't with him when he hit the oak tree. It's my fault."

Alisha felt that Jason's titanic ego had sunk him and there wasn't a thing Jessie could have done about it, but she couldn't say that. Even thinking it made her feel a little bit spooked, because somewhere, probably from her grandmother, she'd heard it was bad luck to think ill of the dead.

All she said was, "Am I understanding you right? These days your mother won't talk to you at all unless you dress up like Jason?"

"Right."

Alisha leaned forward to touch her friend's hand. "Jessie, that is so wrong. I'm sorry; you know I like your mother, but this time she's *wrong*."

"She's grieving," Jessie said, a little angry, a little defensive.

"Sure, but there are limits. Listen, I have an idea. Please think about this, Jessie—it might really be the answer. You could go live with your father for a while."

"What?" Jessie jolted upright as if Alisha had stuck a needle into her. "My *father*?"

"Yeah." It took Alisha some effort to say this, because she knew how Jessie blamed her father for the divorce. She said he never phoned her and she refused to phone him, which was weird, considering that, before her father left, she had been so all about him. Back then her father was wonderful to her and took her side when she got into fights with her mother. Alisha remembered Mr. Ressler as a handsome, all-American kind of guy, nice and mellow even when he drank too much. He liked to hang around bars, and he certainly was the kind who was attracted to women and women to him. Which maybe explained why Mrs. Ressler had transferred all her attention and her adoration to Jason.

And now Jason was gone, Alisha reminded herself, feeling a little shaken because, for a moment, she had forgotten he was dead.

Jessie was saying, "My *father* didn't even bother to come to Jason's f-f-funeral. . . ."

Before Jessie could start crying, Alisha grabbed her by the arm and said, "What if he didn't know? What if nobody *told* him?"

"But—I—how . . ." Sitting with her mouth open, Jessie looked more like herself and less like Jason than Alisha had seen her all day.

Alisha challenged, "Listen, Jessie, your mother is not acting rational. Even at the funeral she was still saying it was all a mistake, like, the casket was empty, and Jason would be coming back. Do you really think she phoned your father to tell him Jason was dead?"

"Don't go there, okay?" Jessie scowled. "There's no reason she should phone Dad about anything. And I won't phone him, either. He wouldn't help me if he could."

"What makes you think that?"

"Dad is—just—he would blame me, too."

"Why?"

"Because I should have stayed with Jason."

"Jessie, that makes no sense! Listen, call your father. Please?"

"No. Why should I call him when he never calls me? I need to stay here."

"Why?"

"Just because."

"Are you staying with your Mom or not letting go of Jason?"

"Whatever."

Alisha sat with her fists clenched, fighting to keep her voice calm. "Does staying here include wearing Jason's clothes?"

"I can wear what I want. There's no law—"

"Jessie, how long are you going to keep this up?"

"As long as I damn well like!" Leaving her lunch, Jessie got up and walked away, her chin high and her shoulders hard.

Alisha couldn't eat. She couldn't even see her lunch tray through the blur in her eyes. *Don't give up*, she commanded herself, clenching her teeth, refusing to let the tears fall. Jessie had always been there for her. Jessie was the only one who would sit with her that first month of middle school. Jessie had gone clothes shopping with her. Jessie had helped her with her English papers. *Don't give up on her now that she needs help.*

Chapter Seven

When Jessie swaggered in from school, Mom was waiting in her shopping clothes—knit top and slacks—instead of her usual housedress. With a big smile on her face, she waved a check. "The life insurance money came through," she said. "What kind of car should we get?"

Jessie didn't give a rat's hind end about cars, but she knew what Jason would say. He had talked about it all the time. "A Z-car. Nissan."

"Okay, let's go shopping!"

Not Jessie's idea of fun. She mumbled almost in her own voice, "Um, I have a lot of homework to do."

"Sweetie! Homework can wait!"

"Okay. Um, yeah, yeah."

They took the check to the bank in town first, then headed for the main highway out to the sprawling car lots. Jessie drove because Mom was nervous behind the wheel. Yet Mom didn't like being a passenger, either. She sat clutching both armrests. Jessie handled the rental car carefully, trying not to spook Mom, and as they approached the Nissan dealer Mom exclaimed, "Sweetie, I had no idea you were such a good driver! You deserve the very best car we can get you."

"Yeah, yeah."

From tagging along with her father, Jessie knew that car

shopping took a long time. Looking around, comparing costs, miles per gallon, style, performance, then price and warranty negotiation—it took forever. But not this time. They walked onto the lot, and Jessie's mom asked, "Which one?"

Not really caring, just being Jason, Jessie pointed toward a row of low, two-seater, sexy-looking sports cars.

"They're *pretty*." Mom started dodging between cars and peering at sticker prices. Jessie wandered from car to car more casually, ever so cool, with her shoulders square and her hands in her pockets. Pretending not to care, still, she was watching her mother. She remembered her father had once told her that the reason she and her mother didn't get along was because they were so much alike. Back then, Dad had loved both Mom and her, so it was okay for him to say they were alike, but Jessie had never really understood. Dad had said they were both perfectionists, both idealists, and neither of them accepted reality very well. Jessie wondered what Dad would think if he saw Mom cooing over these expensive cars.

Anger kicked in. To hell with Dad. He probably had an expensive car, too. If he knew about the insurance money, he would probably want some of it for himself. The amount Jessie had seen printed on the check had been huge. Apparently they paid a lot for dead people.

Dead. Jason.

It hit her in the gut as always. Jessie had to bite her lip to keep from sobbing.

A salesman came out of the showroom. Actually, several sales guys came out and kind of lined up. Jessie noticed they were looking at her as if she freaked them out, but why? These people hadn't known Jason.

"Sweetie!" Mom called after the salesman had talked with her awhile. "Automatic or four on the floor?"

"Four on the floor!" Jessie knew that Jason, who would drive any car anybody would let him get his hands on, had loved to shift gears. Said you could get massively more control that way.

"That's the sports package, then. Which color?"

Jessie opened her mouth and shut it again, struggling within herself. She liked the gold car. She knew Jason would have wanted the black one.

At that moment she overheard someone whisper, "Is that a boy or a girl?"

Anger burning, she knew she had to be Jason. "Black!" she yelled. "Do they have leather interior?" Jessie herself would have preferred plush—the gold car had a sort of grayish-violet plush that was to die for—but she couldn't be herself.

They had leather. Charcoal. Electronically adjustable seats and windows, super lightweight aluminum-alloy wheels, rear spoiler, Bose stereo, and CD player. It was all settled within minutes after Jessie, as Jason, had condescended to stroll over, take a look, and give her okay, even though the sticker price made her blink. Mom got out her checkbook, and the sales guy led her inside the dealership to sign papers. She was in there for maybe ten minutes while Jessie hung around outside. The people who had been staring went away. Nobody spoke to her.

Mom came out with a NISSAN bag full of papers, leather-bound owner's manual, colorful pamphlets. She gave Jessie a frail smile. "I'd like to go home now, Sweetie. I feel as if I need to lie down."

All Mom had to do was look fragile, blink her eyelashes, and almost anybody would do almost anything for her, including

Jessie. This had been true for as long as Jessie could remember. Already a salesman was calling the insurance company, getting them to arrange pickup of the rental car. All Jessie had to do was hand over the keys. Another salesman backed the Z-car out of its tight parking space, pulled up, and stopped in front of Jessie as if he were bringing Cinderella her carriage. The man got out, tried to smile as he looked at her with too much white showing around the rims of his eyes, and gestured her into the driver's seat almost with a bow.

Jessie took her time, adjusting the seat the way she liked it, leaning back a little, and positioning the steering wheel low on her lap, while she studied the instruments. In the passenger seat, Mom yakked, "I've never bought such an expensive car in my life! And it was so easy! Just choose the car and give the people the money!"

"I bet you never bought a car before at all," Jessie teased.

"Well, I guess that's true!"

Turning the key in the ignition, feeling the smooth hum of the Z-car buzz through her body like a soothing massage, Jessie reached for the stick shift and remembered almost as if it didn't matter that, speaking of things people had never done before, she had never driven a four-on-the-floor.

But it was okay. She'd let Jason do it. His presence was with her, kind of inside her, like an instinct. With his guidance, she pressed the clutch, shifted into first gear, eased out the clutch, and the Z-car slid off as smoothly as a black python.

Mom exclaimed, "My, Sweetie, you *do* drive nicely!"

Jessie grunted.

"What would you like for supper, Honey?"

"Dunno. Later." Jessie could hardly wait to drop Mom off at

home and take the new car out by herself. Supper? Forget it. Homework? Ditto. For once in her life, she could skip homework. So what if her grades slipped a little? What would anybody do to her, hang her by her thumbs?

"You're going to take your new toy for a spin? Have fun, darling, and be safe," Mom sang as she got out in front of the house.

The Z-car purred like a big black cat as Jessie drove through town. It growled more like a black lion as she reached a country road and opened it up, running through the gears. The car responded with seemingly limitless power to her slightest pressure on the accelerator, obeyed her slightest turn of the steering wheel. She felt its surefooted tires mastering the road as she swung around curves. She tried rapid acceleration, shifting from first gear straight to third. The car never broke stride. It could do anything. It made her feel as if it were alive and she were part of it, wanting to sink deeper into its strong, swift, wild black depths.

She eased the seat back even more, so that she held the steering wheel low, at arm's length, so that her legs extended full-length to reach the pedals, so that she nearly lounged, like a movie star beside a swimming pool. Jessie had never felt this way about a car. Suddenly and for the first time in her life, she wanted to buy herself some expensive sunglasses. Not to protect her from the sun. To look cool. Brand-name shades.

Acting on impulse—and Jessie did not often act on impulse—she headed off in another direction, drove to a pricey department store she'd been to only a few times before, parked the Z-car at an angle, taking up two spaces, and strolled toward the entrance.

People stared at her shining new black car and stared at her, and she liked it. She felt cool. She wished she were dressed in black jeans and a black hoodie. She'd feel even more cool then.

She took her time at the gleaming racks of sunglasses, looking often in the mirror as she tried on pair after pair of fashionable shades, settling finally on Oakley Flak Jacket Asian Fit, black frames, deep purple lenses. She paid the bill, well over a hundred dollars, with her duplicate of Mom's credit card, meant only for emergencies. Hell, life was an emergency at this point. Yet she felt so no-problem about everything. In fact, she liked living this way, like a spy in a foreign place, wearing a disguise that might betray her.

Even though it was getting dark, she put on the new sunglasses right away, feeling without acknowledging the envious looks some people gave her as she strutted to her new car.

Sweeeet.

She took an indirect way home, driving fast, savoring the way the Z-car handled and cornered. She didn't say a thing to her mother as she walked in the door, sunglasses still on. But Mom beamed a high-wattage smile as she told her to go wash her hands for supper.

Upstairs, laying the Oakleys on top of Jason's dresser, Jessie noticed three other pairs of sunglasses there. Why hadn't she stopped to think Jason had shades already? She'd gone and wasted all that money—but within a moment she shrugged it off. Mom was such a space cadet that she wouldn't notice, or if she did, she wouldn't care. Anyway, it had been fun.

Supper was steak with double-baked cheese potatoes. Jessie had never liked cheese potatoes, but she ate them anyway, and they tasted better than she remembered.

Then instead of doing any homework, she watched TV,

taking charge of the remote before Mom could get to it. She found herself interested in one of those shows about oversize, heavily tattooed men battling each other hand and foot inside what looked like a kind of chain-link fence. She didn't have a clue what they were trying to prove, but it looked like they wanted to kill each other. Interesting.

Mom got up and left the room. "That sort of thing gives me nightmares."

But Jessie didn't have any nightmares. She was sleeping in Jason's bed now, with essence of Jason in the pillow, the blanket, the camouflage-print sheets. She fell asleep right away. And she had a good dream. She dreamed Jason was sitting in the room with her. She saw his handsome face grinning at her. *Way to go, Sis.* She saw him give her thumbs-up. He didn't look like a dead person.

Chapter Eight

As soon as Alisha got out of school, she headed for the post office, where she asked a pimply, red-faced woman behind the counter whether Mr. Ressler had left a forwarding address. She had made up her mind that Jessie's father had to be told what was going on, and she, Alisha, had to tell him. But she didn't have the phone number, and it was no use asking Jessie for it—Jessie had made it pretty clear she wouldn't cooperate. Alisha had no idea where Jessie's father lived now, but she hoped if she could get his forwarding address, she might luck out with a phone number from Information.

The pimply woman repeated, "Mr. Ressler?"

"I don't know his first name."

"Well, you'd better find out, hadn't you?"

It had been over two years since Jessie's father had left, but Alisha remembered he used to work at the State Farm Insurance office, so she trudged down Main Street to ask there.

"Ressler?" said the receptionist, a young woman with a face that looked as if it had been spray-painted around her impossibly green eyes, probably colored contacts. "Ron *Ressler*? He hasn't set foot in here for years."

"Do you know where he moved to?"

"Indianapolis, wasn't it? Or maybe Grand Rapids. Or was it Saint Louis? I can't remember."

"Do you, um, have it on file someplace?"

"I doubt it. Why would we?"

Starting to get blisters on her toes from her new sandals, Alisha trudged back to the post office and asked for the forwarding address of Ron, or Ronald, Ressler.

The pimply, red-faced woman told her, "We don't give out that information. Privacy laws."

Alisha cried, "Why didn't you tell me that in the first place?"

"Don't get smart with me, young lady."

Clamping her mouth shut, Alisha turned to leave. As she went out the door, the woman called after her, "It's been more than a year, anyway. We only keep the forwarding addresses for a year."

So she knew who I was talking about all along, Alisha thought, with a familiar sour feeling swelling in her belly, a kind of emotional indigestion. She wondered whether the woman had treated her that way because she didn't like teenagers, or whether she was hateful to people in general, or whether it was because Alisha was Black. It was hard not to assume the worst, and it was no use asking. She would never know for sure.

She never did know for sure.

Except with Jessie.

Around a corner away from the post office, Alisha plopped onto a park bench, slipped her sore feet out of her sandals, and grabbed her cell phone, aching to talk with Jessie. But she couldn't let Jessie find out she was trying to track down her father. She'd just talk with her. She wanted to hear the sound of her voice. She dialed Jessie's cell phone, but it rang and rang. Five times, six, seven. Finally the voice mail picked up, robotic. "You have reached the mailbox of . . ."

And then Jessie's real voice. "Jessica Ressler."

A sweet, soft voice. Tears stung Alisha's eyes. She clicked off. Couldn't leave a message. Didn't know what in the world to say.

She took a long breath, got up, and got moving again. To the public library this time, to use a computer, since her family didn't have one at home. It was just her, Mom, and Grandmom. Mom worked hard for not much money. Grandmom cooked spicy food and gave out advice, superstitions, and warnings. Such as, don't mess with other people's business. Especially not what she called "funny business."

Alisha saw nothing funny about it. And if she didn't try to help Jessie, who would?

On the computer, she quickly discovered that most of the "Find People" sites wanted money. She tried the Whitepages.com without success. She really needed Ron Ressler's middle initial. She tried MySpace and Facebook and LinkedIn; no luck. Same problem. Time to go low-tech. At the library's reference desk she asked whether they had old phone books for the local area. They did. Looking in the phone book from three years ago, Alisha found that Jessie's father's name was actually "W. Richard Ressler."

Richard, not Ronald. Clueless One at the insurance place had gotten it wrong. Why hadn't the damn woman at the post office corrected her?

It doesn't matter. That woman is a total waste of organs that could be donated. Don't think about her.

W. Richard Ressler. Alisha wondered what the *W* stood for. It was probably something Mr. Ressler didn't like. Walter? Wolfgang? Wilberforce?

I have to start all over.

And she'd wasted so much time. A smart person who had a clue, like a private detective or a cop on TV, would probably be already talking with Jessie's father by now, but Alisha hadn't even gotten to first base. Who the heck did she think she was, a stupid girl trying to be a hero. . . .

Stop it. Don't dis yourself. Just do it.

She'd never stayed at the library so late before. Mom was home by now. Alisha phoned to tell her where she was and said she was working on a school project.

By now Alisha was so hungry it hurt. Also, she had a headache. The computers were crowded, and she had to wait her turn. Once back on, she went to Whitepages.com with the correct name. But still no luck. She tried to find W. Richard Ressler among a listing of State Farm Insurance agents, then insurance agents in general. But she didn't find him there, either, and she didn't even know whether he still worked in insurance. She didn't know much about him at all except gossip about the Ressler divorce. Some people said it was because Mrs. Ressler was kind of selfish and shallow. Other people said it was because Mr. Ressler was inclined to drink and screw around. Probably both things were true. Which came first, the shallow wife or the straying husband?

Well, wherever he was, he was probably still chasing women. Huh.

Alisha went back to the home page and clicked a heading called "Singles."

It was like stepping into the bar district of a strange, sleazy city. Voices calling "Want Me, Want ME!" Advertising loud and louder. Why did these people have to advertise? Did *older* mean *lonely*? The neediness reaching out of the computer screen made Alisha uncomfortable. It took her a while to get things sorted out in her mind. Most of the "Find Your Soul Mate" sites wanted money; she couldn't go on them. Others were so nearly pornographic they warned her away. Still others consisted of classified ads, such as "DWM seeks WF into Rollerblading, boogie-boarding, other athletic pursuits" which did not help her—there was no way of telling whether any of the DWMs were Jessie's father. There was too much to sort through, and it was taking her too long. Sites for certain regions did not help, as Alisha did not know where, geographically, Jessie's father was. Sites that gave only first names but showed photos—

It was a long shot, but Alisha *did* know what Mr. Ressler looked like.

She was scrolling through posed picture after posed picture—*Look, I'm cool, See my style, See my shoulders, See my boobs, See my smile*—and, for the first time in her life, feeling grateful she was still in high school and didn't have to go through this kind of virtual humiliation, when she heard an adult voice speak to her. "Alisha."

One of the librarians.

"Alisha, it's time for you to get off the computer. Other people are waiting."

Of course she had used up her half hour and then some, and of course Alisha didn't talk back because there was nothing to say, but she wanted to scream. Or cry. The next photo could have been Jessie's father.

Yeah, right. Odds about a million to one.

Alisha clicked the computer back to the home page, stood up on legs stiff from sitting, left the library, and trudged toward home, mind-weary, heart-weary, soul-weary. She still hadn't found Jessie's father, and she wasn't going to quit trying, but she felt scared it might already be too late for him to help Jessie.

Chapter Nine

The next morning Jessie made sure to be on time for school, because she wanted everybody to see her purring into the parking lot in the black Z-car. She wore Jason's black American Outfitters T-shirt, his black jeans, and her—or maybe his, really—new black Oakley shades, and she rolled in like a visiting raja, relishing yet ignoring the shouts and squeals of the onlookers.

She parked the car diagonally across two spaces, which was strictly against the rules. Walking tall, she wore her sunglasses into school, also against the rules. The other kids kept their distance from her and watched her silently, acting more impressed now than hostile. No shouts of "pervert." Instead, one of Jason's teammates from wrestling, a tall, broad-shouldered blond boy named Shane, walked up to her. Jessie'd had a crush on Shane, who was her age, since middle school. Mutely she adored him almost as much as she had adored Jason. He had never noticed her, had never spoken to her before, and she had never spoken to him.

Now here came Shane calling, "Hey, um, *Jason*." He said the name like *yeah, right,* but he was smiling. Challenging, yet not unfriendly.

As if in a dream, Jessie could not feel the floor under her feet. Yet she did what she had to do, answering promptly in her Jason voice, "Yo, Shane, 'sup?"

"That's what I want to know. What's up."

Jessie answered only with a smile. Shane's smile pulled it out of her while she struggled against it, so it may have looked like a girly smile or it may have looked more like a boy smile.

It seemed to puzzle Shane. He loomed over her, scowling. "Let's see how Jason you really are. Dead End Bend tonight at dark, all right?"

Jessie shrugged. "Yeah, yeah."

"Yeah, yeah," Shane mimicked, turning to walk away. "I'll believe it when I see it," he shot over his shoulder as he left.

Jessie felt her heart pumping honey. Shane, talking to her! Interested in her! Life had never been so exciting before.

And it continued that way. The minute she walked into homeroom, the teacher ordered, "Take off those sunglasses, *Miss* Ressler."

Jessie stared. Instead of her usual homeroom teacher, it was Coach, the one who had made her cringe at the door on her first day dressed as Jason. If it weren't for that memory, Jessie might have taken off the sunglasses like a good girl. Really, she knew, she was still Jessie and she needed to make good grades and stay out of trouble. But the way Coach said "*Miss* Ressler" made it sound like being Jessie was equivalent to being a garden slug. She did not answer, only shrugged and slouched back in her desk chair, arms crossed over her chest, chin up, grinning defiance the way Jason might have.

"Jessica Ressler! I'll give you one more chance. Remove your expensive but nonfunctional eyewear."

Ooooh, sarcasm, ooooooh, so scaaaaary it made Jessie laugh.

The teacher said between clenched teeth, "Report to the office, Miss Ressler."

What the hell, she thought as she swaggered out. She would have ended up in trouble sooner or later because of the way she'd parked the Z-car.

In the office, they had her sit and wait for quite a while. Maybe they were trying to make her sweat, but they just made her bored and irritated.

Or maybe they were trying to figure out what to do about her. When she was finally called in, it was not to the principal's office, or the vice principal's. A secretary took her all the way back to the school's "life wellness" office.

The psychologist's office.

Which meant they thought she needed psychiatric help. They thought she was crazy.

Jessie found herself facing one of those ultra-thin, fashionable, aging ladies terrified of their own wrinkles, whose attention to her face—plastic surgery, Botox?—did nothing for the baggy, sagging skin of her neck. "Good morning, Jessie," she said with a show of unnaturally white teeth. She was probably trying to be warm, gentle, reassuring, to project the message *You're not in trouble after all, Jessie. I'm your friend.*

Yeah, right. Jessie just gave a Jason-grunt and slumped in a chair.

"Please take your sunglasses off, dear. I need to be able to see your eyes."

Jessie couldn't really explain why she was getting so annoyed with everything. Before today, she had never worn sunglasses indoors. They were making her world awfully dark, yet she did not want to take them off, because the fun of messing with people's minds more than made up for the inconvenience. She challenged, "Why?"

"So I can try to tell how you're feeling, dear. Why you're acting this way."

"What way?"

The psychologist's warm-and-gentle pose began to erode. "Jessica, you know perfectly well what I'm talking about. Your dressing this way to assume your sadly expired brother's identity is particularly concerning. Allowances have been made for you because grief takes many forms, but now it is time for this to stop."

"According to what calendar?" Jessie shot back. *Skinny old bag, she pisses me off.* Jessie had never felt so angry.

"According to common sense, Jessica. The school administration—"

Jessie jumped out of her chair. "Don't give me that. There's no law—"

The woman leaned forward with what was probably meant to be compassion but felt more like the pity of a superior being dispensing wisdom. "We all have to deal with reality, Jessie."

Anorexia lady thinks I'm crazy just for wearing Jason's clothes? Fine, Jessie decided, she'd be crazy. "That's not my name," she said loudly. "Jason. Call me Jason."

"Now, Jessie, you know we can't do that."

Why not? Jessica, super-student, knew that by law, as long as she wasn't committing a crime she could use whatever name she wanted to. "Call me *Jason*."

The argument went on for some time and ended in a deadlock. Jessie kept her sunglasses on. Jessie said her name was Jason. The school psychologist finally let her go back to class, and for the rest of the day when she wrote her name on her papers, she put Jason Ressler. It looked funny in her neat, oval handwriting instead of his wild scrawl.

Coincidentally, on that same day in a small city several hundred miles away, W. Richard Ressler was also seeing a psychologist, to whom he confided, "It's Wendell. Wendell Richard."

"Nothing wrong with that," the comfortably plump woman responded.

"I know that now, but when I was in school—kids can be awfully cruel about nothing. Wendell Witchie! Wendell Witchie! I hated it."

"They bullied you? Over a period of several years?"

"Oh, yeah. They threw me on the ground and rubbed my face in the dirt whenever they felt like it."

"We're just starting to realize how much that sort of childhood abuse by peers is internalized, contributing to a lifetime lack of self-esteem. It's no wonder you are still trying to find yourself."

Yeppers. And he had gone about it all the wrong ways at first. Leaving his wife and family. Running here, running there, thinking he would feel like a different person in a different place. Bars and fast cars and liquor and drugs, months of partying, until he had ended up in detox. He'd pretty much wasted two years, but now he was clean and trying to stay that way.

He didn't have to tell the doctor any of this; she knew. He'd been seeing her awhile.

"I've been holding down a job and mostly stable for almost six months now," he remarked.

"And?" She smiled at him.

"And I've been thinking—maybe . . ."

"Go on."

"I feel almost ready to face my kids now." Damn, what a fool he'd been. He wouldn't go off the deep end ever again if he could just have his children back in his life. The divorce had given him visitation rights, of course, but try telling that to his ex. She never called to let him know how his son and daughter were doing, and when he tried to phone her, or them, his call was blocked. He had called from other numbers only to have her hang up on him. And she was always the one to answer the phone. Always had been. The house was her domain, and she reigned there.

For the same queen-of-her-small-realm reason, she was always the one to bring in the mail. He had written to both Jason and Jessie several times, but he felt sure they had not received the letters, because he had never heard back from either of them. When he tried to call them on their cell phones, he got a wonking voice telling him the numbers were no longer in service. Probably their doting mother had upscaled them to BlackBerries or something, and even their own father had no way of finding out their numbers.

"I believe I suggested you should contact a lawyer to help you insist on your parental rights?"

"Um, yeah, but I haven't done it yet."

"Why not?"

"I—I want to get past that six-month mark." Then he'd feel strong enough, he hoped. Damn, probably both the kids thought he didn't care about them anymore. No way could they have any idea how badly he wanted to contact them if he could just feel a little steadier on his feet. This was Jessie's senior year. She might very well be her class valedictiorian, and he *would* be there for her graduation—it was a promise he had made to himself and, although she didn't yet know it, to her. Plus, he could hardly wait to see Jason again.

Jason. What a son! Strong, and knew what he wanted from the first day he stood on his feet. You could bet Jason had never been bullied the way his father had been. One hell of a wrestler, and the best-looking boy in town, and the kid had probably been in the pants of every girl in the high school by now. Damn, it was hard not to be rooster-proud of Jason, although Mr. Ressler realized guiltily that he ought to worry, to hope the boy didn't get a girl pregnant or leave a trail of abortions and broken hearts. Because, to tell the truth, Jason wouldn't care. Jason was about as self-centered as they come, what with the way his mother had spoiled him. Mr. Ressler had seen this, but he'd never had the heart to try to reduce the magnitude of Jason's ego, so much the opposite of his own. He adored his son. There was something larger-than-life about Jason.

And Jessie adored Jason the same way, but what was more important, Jessie had adored *him*, her father, when he was still in her life.

The therapist was saying, "Do you really think an arbitrary date will make that much difference?"

"I—I can't delay much longer, I know, but I need to feel ready."

"The word 'stalling' comes to mind. You may never feel ready. Don't you think your children love you regardless?"

"I, um, yes, I guess so, but I don't want to do anything that would make them ashamed of me."

"Why would you? Weren't you a good father before?"

"I tried to be." Especially with Jessie, taking her on father-daughter "dates" to the zoo or a movie, plus ice cream or pizza, trying to make up for the way the little girl's mother just didn't take much interest in her. It made him ache to the core when he thought about her, when he missed her and realized how badly she must miss him. And how she was probably still trying her darnedest to win her mother's love, when the sad truth was there just wasn't much love *there*—except for Jason.

Meanwhile, it had fallen to him to parent Jessie. Help her select modest clothes to wear. Buy her classy jewelry, real ruby, her birthstone. Talk to her about boys, how to be careful, how not to get sweet-talked into trouble. His daughter had a real good reputation, and she was *smart*, a genuine scholar, and even though all that brain was certainly no way to impress her clueless mother, it made Daddy really proud of his little girl, almost as proud as he was of Jason.

His therapist was watching him. "What are you thinking?"

"How much I love those kids."

"They probably believe you deserted them. When are you going to set the law on your ex and get back in touch with them?"

"Every time I think about my ex, I want a drink."

"I know how that is. You just deal with it, that's all." She paused. "I also know it's nice to dream about how wonderful it'll be to see the kids, right? And maybe you're scared to leave the dream behind and face the reality?"

She was right. In his imagination, Jessie and Jason were just the way he had left them. He didn't want to think anything might have changed.

"Don't you think it's time to man up?" his counselor challenged. "Anything could be happening to your children."

*   *   *

When school let out, Alisha went straight to the public library to continue her search for W. Richard Ressler, starting where she had left off yesterday. She looked at every photograph on the singles dating sites, but she could not find him. And even if she did, would he be able to bring Jessie back to being Jessie?

Chapter Ten

After school, Jessie hung around in the lobby, pretending not to watch kids gawk at her new car. It was still parked diagonally. Maybe worn out from dealing with Jessie, the office staff hadn't said anything about it all day. But while the administration ignored the Z-car, some of the kids were practically kissing it. They were still avoiding Jessie herself, and some of them walked past the black beauty trying not to look as if they were eyeing it, but others clustered around it, stroking its sleek hood, stooping to peer into its tinted windows, owlish looks of awe on their faces as they exchanged comments with one another.

Jessie watched, smiled, got bored, idly pulled Jason's cell phone from her pocket, and flipped it open. The instant it lit up, her heart turned over because she knew she was making a mistake, just asking for grief by snooping to see what her dead brother had on his phone. Turn it off, quick—

Wait a minute. It said there were new text messages.

Maybe from the day he had died? Messages he had never answered?

Aching, Jessie knew she had no choice. Pain if she looked, pain and regret if she didn't. She thumbed the button.

And stared. The phrase "stark, staring mad" shot through her mind, and for an instant she wondered what "stark" meant, anyway.

The messages were not from ten days ago, when Jason was killed. They were received today.

Lcum bak J
Who u think u r
DEB r ded
2nite DEB r u chikn
Scrw u + ur car

Jessie couldn't tell from the initials who had sent them. Nothing made sense. Why were they texting him? He was dead. Why about Deb? Who was Deb?

Wait. DEB.

Dead End Bend.

Challenge.

Confrontation.

Her brother's friends daring her to show them that she had a right to go around pretending to be Jason.

Not that it was any of their business, Jessie reminded herself. She didn't care what anybody else thought. She had never cared what kids in school thought of her. A few times in the past, some imbecile had insulted her to her face, calling her a nerd or geek or whatever. Her response had been to turn and walk away. People like that, no matter how crappy they made her feel, were not worth bothering with.

But these commonsense thoughts did Jessie no good. She felt her heart pounding, her neck going hot, her fists clenching, and she knew why: it wasn't about her. She was nobody. But Jason was—had been—somebody, and this was about Jason.

Jason's legend.

Jason's daredevil legacy.

Jason's right to a brand-new, expensive black sports car.

Jessie's blood burned with a new glad-mad defiance even stronger than the anger she had felt in the school psychologist's office. Yes, she would show up at Dead End Bend tonight. Maybe confronting the challengers would put a stop to some of the ugliness in school, she told herself, but even without that rationalization, she would do it anyway.

And she was looking forward to it. She had never felt so bone-deep excited in her whole polite, boring little life. *Thank you, Jason,* she thought, because this rush felt like her brother's gift to her from the grave.

Alisha truly could not think what more to do, but she would not stop trying to locate Jessie's father. Wandering around town, she started looking for adults about the right age and asking them at random. The guy in the hardware store: "Do you know where Mr. Ressler lives now? Yeah, Richard Ressler, do you know where he went when he moved out—no? Never mind. Thanks anyway." Woman in the coffee shop, same thing, guy in the auto-parts store—Alisha realized she was wasting her time, but also it had come to her where she should be asking: the bars.

Not her idea of fun.

Scared her, actually.

But she had to try.

By now it was almost nighttime, and the bars were beginning to fill. As she entered the first one, the bartender took one look at her and said, "Honey, you ain't old enough to come in here."

"I'm just trying to find out where Richard Ressler moved to."

For some reason a few laughs went up from around the room. "Dick? Detox," one guy said.

"Playboy Bunnyland," said another.

The bartender said, "Move along, young lady."

No sooner had she stepped onto the sidewalk outside when her cell phone rang. It was her mother. "Alisha, where the heck are you?"

Tired of lying, she told the truth, sort of. "Downtown."

"Downtown! What for?"

"Trying to find out where Mr. Ressler is."

"Find out where Mr. Ressler is? Why?"

Alisha heard a screech from her grandmother. "You tell that girl she riling the spirits, riling the spirits! You tell her she sticking her hand in ghost snake's nest!"

Ignoring this, Alisha pleaded, "Mom, if I could get him to talk to Jessie—"

"If I could get you to mind your own business! You come on home *right now*!"

Alisha walked toward a bus stop, telling herself that she would try again tomorrow. But she felt like crying, because tomorrow might be too late.

She heard footsteps behind her.

Stiffening, she stopped and turned.

A man was ambling out of the bar. Old guy who somehow reminded her of a white rabbit, maybe because of his white fuzz of beard and hair. Maybe more because of his weak face. Harmless looking. Although never relaxing completely, Alisha stood still and let him walk up to her. He handed her a dirty napkin on which was inked a phone number.

"Rick Ressler's cell," he mumbled, his speech a bit slurred, his breath reeking of beer. Clownishly, he smiled. "Didn't want the guys to see me. Ruin my reputation of being no good for anything." He meandered down the sidewalk while Alisha stared after him, so surprised she didn't even think to say thank you.

After he disappeared around the corner, she jumped, coming out of her daze. Muttering "Duh!" at herself, she grabbed her cell phone. With a shaking hand she fingered the numbers.

Right around dark, Jessie got into the black Z-car, revved it, and zoomed off into the twilight, heading toward Dead End Bend.

There had been no need to come up with a story to tell her mother. Jason had always done what he wanted, and Jessie was being Jason. She had just said, "See ya, Mud," on her way out the door.

Now, driving across town, she kept finding herself getting lead-footed. She kept trying to slow down to somewhere near the speed limit, but it was as if the Z-car had a mind of its own. It *wanted* to go fast.

Almost out of town, heading through the commercial strip of video rentals, Kwik-Marts, pizza places, and burger joints, Jessie heard a siren bleep, looked in the rearview mirror, and saw the flashing lights of the police car behind her.

She pulled over and stopped at once, thinking with amusement, *Going too fast past the fast food.* Jessie had never been stopped by the police, and she had always thought that she would just *die* if she ever got a ticket. But for some reason now she didn't care. Maybe since Jason was dead, dumb stuff like speeding tickets didn't seem so important anymore. Jessie felt cool, like this wasn't even worth getting nervous about, like it might be fun. She pressed the button that rolled her window down, took off her sunglasses, and laid her hands in plain sight on the hub of the steering wheel, but she felt herself grinning.

Another police car pulled in front of her. The first cop had called for backup? Sweet!

Now the police officer parked behind her walked up to her window, and when he looked at her, something seemed to bother him. He stared, his face taut and gray. In robotic tones he said, "Driver's license and registration, please."

Jason had no driver's license, only a learner's permit, so Jessie handed over her own license along with the pink paper that served as temporary registration for the new car.

The cop looked at her driver's license, glared at her and said, "You look just like that dead punk, freak me out, and now you hand me a *girl's* license?"

"That's me," Jessie said in her normal, soft voice. "I've changed my hair, that's all." But she couldn't seem to stop grinning.

The other cop had come over. "Wipe that stupid grin off your face."

Jessie had to wipe it off literally, smoothing both hands across her cheeks and mouth. "Honestly, I'm not trying to be smart," she said quietly before they could react to the gesture.

"What do you make of this?" The first cop passed her driver's license to the other.

"Jessie Ressler, huh?" The second cop studied her. "You Jason Ressler's sister?"

Suddenly Jessie's throat closed on her voice. She nodded.

The first cop said suddenly, "Yeah, you're a girl, okay. I see it." Either he had been checking her narrow shoulders, her barely visible boobs, or he could tell now by the look on her face. "Young lady, I don't know what to ask you first, why you're going sixty in a thirty-five-miles-an-hour zone, or why you're dressed like . . ."

"Just let it go," muttered the other cop, grudging sympathy in his eyes.

"The speeding, or the cross-dressing?"

"You do what you want about the speeding."

The cop who had stopped Jessie asked her, "Did you know how fast you were going?"

"Yes, sir. I can't seem to help it. This car just wants to go fast." Jessie was starting to smile again.

"Kid like you shouldn't be driving that car. You know I ought to give you a citation. You could end up with a big fat fine and points on your driving record."

"I know. It's okay."

"Okay? What do you mean, okay?" The cop was getting worked up.

"I just mean I take responsibility."

"For the speeding or the cross-dressing?"

The other cop put in quietly, "She's dressed like her dead brother. Might be some sort of coping thing."

"Well, I can't cope with it! This whole thing's too damn Twilight Zone for me." He thrust Jessie's license and registration back at her. "Girl, I'm letting you off with a warning. I don't ever want to see you again. Shut your mouth, don't say a word to me, and get out of here."

Jessie did as instructed. Although she did not actually lay a patch, unmistakably she exhibited excess speed as she pulled away. And she managed to get only a short distance down the road before laughter exploded from her. Driving fast, faster, she laughed and kept laughing, louder.

Chapter Eleven

Shane already had things set up down at Dead End Bend. He had stuck a homemade bright-red bandanna flag in the shoulder of the road on the downward slope, and directly opposite on the upward slope, another flag. Distance between the flags, exactly half a mile. The turn was so tight that both flags could be observed by one guy with a stopwatch who stood in the middle of the vacant field in between. The contestant's speed in miles per hour around Dead End Bend could be figured by the time it took him to do half a mile between the two flags. They didn't teach math at school for nothing.

Shane was of course the guy with the stopwatch, and Alisha stood nearby. In fact, Shane had brought her down there with him in his pickup truck. Alisha had been standing near the bus stop but not quite at it, not wanting to go home and face her mother's anger and her grandmother's voodoo pits full of ghost snakes, when Shane had pulled over and offered her a ride.

"Thanks," she had said, getting in, and then, because it mattered so much she had to tell somebody, she blurted, "Guy from the bar came after me and gave me the phone number."

"Huh?"

"Jessie's father's phone number. I called him about five times."

"Jessie's father!"

"Yeah. But he's not answering. I keep getting his voice mail, and it cuts me off after about three seconds. Not that I know what to say to him anyway."

Amazingly, Shane seemed to follow. "I don't know what the hell *anybody* can say."

Alisha wondered if Shane had any clue about Jessie's crush on him. Jessie had good taste. Shane seemed like a super-nice guy as well as a hunk. Jeez, just when Alisha thought life couldn't get much weirder, here she was in Shane's pickup truck. Poor Jessie; she would be jealous if she were in her right mind.

Alisha said softly, "I have to try to call again. Later tonight. I have to try to do something."

At Dead End Bend, standing in the bed of Shane's pickup truck parked in the field, Alisha watched others arriving. Word had gotten around even faster than usual. There were plenty of kids interested. Like, *really* interested, wanting to see whether Jessie would show up. Those who planned to compete waited along the roadside uphill from the starting flag. Those who wanted to watch bumped through a ditch and over ruts and grass to park in the field. Whoever owned this land had put up fences that had been torn down, placed concrete barriers that had been pushed away, and had finally given up trying to keep the kids out. The people in the few neighboring houses had likewise gotten tired of calling the cops, who never showed up in time anyway. This night, this wasteland, this unobstructed view of Dead End Bend belonged to the teenagers.

Kids sat on the hoods or tops of their cars, talking, joking, flirting, or play-fighting, drinking soda or beer, smoking cigarettes or joints. Some, like Alisha, kept a watch on the cars lining up to compete, more or less visible in the glare of one another's headlights. When Alisha saw the Z-car blacker than the night coming down the hill, she was not the only one who exclaimed aloud. But she *was* the only one who took off running, running out of the field and up the road to try to talk with her best friend.

Tinted glass in the windows made the black car like a hooded thing, impenetrable. When Alisha knocked on the driver's-side window and it rolled down, she was still facing tinted glass she could not see into, Jessie's expensive eyeglasses on a hard face that might as well have been Jason's.

"Jessie," Alisha appealed, "what are you doing?"

"What's it look like?" The hard voice was Jason's.

"Please, Jessie, talk like yourself."

"Yeah, yeah."

"Please!"

"Okay, Alisha." Jessie's face softened along with her voice. "Would you stop worrying about me so much? I'm all right."

Alisha didn't think so. "You're going to try to run Dead End Bend?"

"Yes. So Jason's friends will let up on me."

"But, Jessie, are you really going to push the car?"

"Of course."

"But you can't!"

"Who says?"

"I mean, you know what could happen!" How could Jessie, who was so smart, intend to do the same stupid thing that had gotten her brother killed? But Alisha found herself reluctant, no, afraid, really afraid, to speak of Jason, as if mentioning him might be bad luck. "Jessie," she appealed, "do you *want* to crash?"

Jessie breathed out through puffed lips as if dealing with a dense kindergartener. She spoke with exaggerated patience. "I won't crash. I won't get hurt. I won't get killed."

"What makes you so sure?"

"I just know. Alisha, stop bothering me and get out of here."

"The hell I will. I'm coming with you." Alisha started toward the passenger-side door.

"*No.*" The hard voice also might as well have been Jason's. With a click of a switch, Jessie locked both car doors, then said more softly, "Alisha, don't be an idiot. He'll protect me, but he won't protect you."

Alisha froze, staring at the dark surface of a pair of sunglasses that might have hidden anyone's eyes, unable to force her voice through her throat to whisper, "What do you mean?"

She couldn't speak the words. Because she didn't really have to ask what Jessie meant. She knew.

"Protect?" she wanted to cry. "You call it protection?"

But she could not bear what she was thinking. It was crazy, impossible. She could not face Jessie another moment. Blindly she turned away from her friend and ran back into the night.

Jessie's laughter after the cops had pulled her over had spun out of the dark joke at the core of her recent life, irony she hadn't appreciated before that moment. Jessie the perfectionist had done very little giggling in her life. Jessie the idealist had taken everything very seriously. Jessie the scholar had even looked up "stark" in the library after school today. "Stark" meant stiff like starch, severe, grim, and also rigid like a dead body.

But Jessie speeding the powerful car toward danger along the country road laughed out loud with delight that she felt no need for any of the usual Jessie worries. She laughed because she was not Jessie right now; she was Jason, and therefore she could not possibly get killed, *because Jason was already dead.* So what was the worst that could happen?

Waiting at Dead End Bend, she wanted to go strutting over to Shane, but she was sure to go all blushy girl if she tried to really talk with him, and she couldn't let that happen yet. Maybe later tonight, or tomorrow. Wow, he had finally noticed her; he was finally talking to her! Her whole life was changing so fast—

The first car got moving. Jessie watched intently as a yellow Firebird zoomed back up the road to get a good start, then came tearing down past the red-bandanna flag, flashed its brake lights briefly before entering the bend, revved, spun out onto the wide gravel shoulder, fishtailed, managed to get itself lined up with the ascending road, and roared uphill past the finish flag. The kids watching clapped and cheered. Good run.

The next car drifted around the bend like a racecar cornering but took no chances. Average run.

By this time, Jessie noticed, the yellow car had returned and parked on the grass. The boy who was driving had gotten out and was talking with Shane, probably finding out his time. Then he joined some friends sitting on another car, watching. Someone gave him a pat on the back.

The next car whizzed past Jessie, went into Dead End Bend fast, spun, couldn't pull out of the spin, did a 180, and jammed on the brakes to stop before it ran off the gravel into the trees. Disqualified. The great oak that had taken Jason shadowed it. At the tree's base, visible in the headlights as the car made its shuddering stop, stood a four-foot homemade white wooden cross.

Jessie started watching not the cars, but the cross that caught their headlights as they approached Dead End Bend: Jason's cross marking the heart of the danger. Shadowed, then shining white, then shadowed again in the gloom of the oak, then once more bright in the headlights. Stuffed animals—teddy bears, woolly lambs, white unicorns, bright red Tasmanian devils—at its base. She could not see them at this distance, but she knew what they were. She *could* see a wreath of white flowers hanging on the cross like a choker necklace.

Jason wouldn't like that, a necklace. And he had never liked flowers. And he pretty much hated stuffed animals.

Staring at Jason's cross, Jessie did not even realize it was her turn until her foot stomped on the accelerator and her hands spun the wheel, swerving her onto the road. She did not go uphill to get a good start. No need. The Z-car did zero to sixty in—

Sixty?

Stark terror seized Jessie. White cross getting big bigger and blazing white, so white she blinked even behind her Oakley shades, wavering fiery white and almost as huge as the dark oak tree towering. The oak tree. This was crazy. Please, no, she did not want to die. Jessie tried to hit the brakes.

Something wouldn't let her.

It was the same something that had shown her how to drive a stick shift. The presence she had kept to herself until now—but here, at Dead End Bend, the only way she could come out alive was if she let Jason take over completely. Let him take total control. Heck, he had already taken over. Jessie knew she might have the body of a girl but really she was like Luke Skywalker using the Force; she was her brother's sister-self, she was inhabited and aided by a supernatural boy, and as her car spun into the curve, her fear spun beyond terror into a long ascending spiral of ecstasy. Jason was here! Jason lounged in the seat; Jason gripped the wheel; Jason pressed the accelerator. Leaving her along the dark road that awful night a week and a half ago, Jason had said he would come back for her, and now he had done it! He had come back because he loved her the way she loved him; he had to. He would never let anything bad happen to her. She was invincible.

Chapter Twelve

Alisha stayed around only because she needed a ride home with Shane. She stood near him yet felt all alone in the crowd watching from the grassy slope. Shivering in the warm night, she wrapped her arms tight around herself, trying to hold together.

She saw Jessie in the Z-car take off like a black tornado. She didn't hear everybody screaming, because she was screaming too, screaming herself deaf, watching the black car swerve off the road toward the trees, not even trying to make the bend, wrong, all wrong, deadly! Why hadn't she thought, why hadn't she realized that Jessie was suicidal and meant to die? Why hadn't she *known*?

Alisha couldn't scream anymore; she couldn't catch her breath. She couldn't watch. Shutting her eyes tight, she bowed her head, hands over her face, shuddering.

But in that instant the screams all around her turned to shouts, yells, and Alisha smelled scorching rubber, and as her head came up and her eyes opened like sunrise, she saw the black car slew almost impossibly sideways and hit the white cross, avoiding the big oak tree by inches but knocking down the cross and running it over as the tires spun in the dirt, as the car drifted into a perfect line to take the uphill slope. Alisha heard thunder, the Z-car's engine thunder and the thunder of leaping, stamping feet and pounding hands. And she saw lightening—but no, there couldn't have been lightning. She saw Jessie's Z-car barreling up the other side of the bend, safe, thank God, safe, and as it flashed past—nothing made sense, there must have been lightning, because for a blue-strobe moment she saw. Everyone saw.

Oakley shades.

Grinning face.

Hand, waving.

Then the car passed by.

In a weird silence the crowd of teenagers listened to the roar of its engine fading into the distance. It was not coming back.

Shane was the first to speak. He whispered, "That was Jason."

Alisha said numbly, "No." But her reply was lost in the hubbub all around as the group lost its purpose, its cohesion, and broke to pieces. Some kids headed for their cars as if all they wanted was to get out of there. Some clung to one another. One nerd asked what Jason's, or rather Jessie's, time had been. Shane didn't know. He hadn't clicked the stopwatch.

In the same stunned whisper he said, "Jason. Took out that cross. On purpose."

Several kids had run across Dead End Bend to look at the shattered cross with ghoulish zest, as if it were a hit-and-run victim—but even from the distance, Alisha could see how they stiffened and stopped in their tracks. One of them screamed, "There's nothing here!"

"Whatcha mean?" somebody from the other side of the road shouted back.

"I mean *nothing!* Not even a piece of wood! Not even the stump!"

Alisha appealed, "Shane, please take me home."

But he was already jogging away from her, downhill and across the road to the place where the cross wasn't.

Where the white flowers were not. Or the teddy bears. Or the angel dolls. Nothing.

Alisha did not go down there. She climbed into Shane's pickup truck's cab, lay down on the seat, and curled up, hugging her own knees. She lay like that for a long time.

She said nothing to Shane when he came back. She didn't sit up or look at him. He said nothing to her as he started the pickup and drove very slowly, very carefully, back to town.

After her final blast of speed in the Z-car, Jessie slowed down, too, because her hands started wobbling on the wheel and her vision blurred. She felt limp, physically weak, shaken, aching all over as if she had been in a fight or—maybe this was what it felt like to give birth, so utterly exhausted and joyous. Jason's name sang in her mind, Jason, Jason had saved her. Jason had saved her life. Only his force of will surging through her and turning the steering wheel with more physical strength and skill than she possessed had kept her from smashing into the oak. She vaguely remembered a small crash, like she had run over something, but so what? She had rounded Dead End Bend on four screeching tires and had left it alive, at top speed, and victorious in Jason's love. That was all that mattered.

So wiped out that she stumbled as she walked, she let herself into the dark house, staggered upstairs, and collapsed onto her bed in her clothes. Rather, she collapsed onto Jason's bed in Jason's clothes. Whatever.

She slept like a dead person.

Dreamless.

Motionless.

Not long enough. The alarm clock rang far too early.

She forced herself to get up for school—thank God it was Friday—so bleary and nearly asleep on her feet that she did not even brush her teeth or look in the mirror to spike her hair with her fingers. She just stumbled down to breakfast still in the same clothes as the day before.

And there was Mom piling corn pancakes hot from the skillet onto a platter. Jessie felt her stomach respond with a rumble of hunger, her mouth with a smile as she sat down and dug into a short stack of three pancakes with butter and maple syrup. Yum. Corn pancakes were her favorite—

Wait a minute. They were Jason's favorite. Jessie had never particularly liked them.

Well, maybe it was just because she was so hungry that they tasted good. She couldn't remember when she had felt so cavernously hungry. As she gulped down the pancakes in big bites, Mom brought her another stack, then sat down to sip coffee, smiling at her.

Mom said, "You were out late last night. Showing off the new car? With your friends?"

Jessie gave a nod and a grunt.

"We really have to get your driver's license, Sweetie. Sooner or later the cops are going to stop you."

They already had. Jessie smiled to herself, thinking about that poor belligerent cop trying to wrap his slow mind around a "punk kid" who looked like a boy and drove like a boy but had a girl's slim body, pert little breasts, slender manicured hands.

"You're going to be late for school," Mom said.

"Yeah, yeah."

As Jessie headed out the door, her mother gave her a swat on the butt. Mom had never done that to her before. Just to Jason. Jessie felt her heart swell. It felt so good to be her mom's pet, to finally be—go ahead and think it—loved. It was hard to believe that only five days ago she had been a miserable, mousy, grieving girl whose own mother wouldn't speak to her. And that she had been smart or desperate enough to come up with this Jason game. Now she laughed at cops, laughed at teachers, wasn't afraid of anything—she had to give herself credit. Her life was so much better since—

"Wait a minute," Mom said.

Pausing on her way out the door, Jessie turned back to her mother, who stood studying her in the light from outside.

Mom reached up to stroke Jessie's face. "Son," she said with proud love in her voice, "you're growing up. You're going to have to start shaving soon."

Jessie lifted her hand and felt prickly hairs growing out of her chin.

Chapter Thirteen

Jessie drove to school in a daze, her mind spinning. She could pluck the chin hairs out when it was time, or wax them off, or there were other ways, laser surgery—

Rounding a corner a little too fast for safety, she noticed her own hand on the steering wheel, her own flexed wrist and muscular lower arm, like a sculpture by Michelangelo, so beautiful in the sunlight, strong tendons of her fingers and perfect—

Just like the hand and arm she had seen sprawling out from under the wrecked red Mustang.

"No," she whispered.

What was the first stage of grief? Denial?

"No!" she said fiercely out loud.

Reaching school, she parked in a single space instead of diagonally across two. What the hell, the Z-car was scratched up anyway from whatever she had hit last night. She got out, started walking across the parking lot toward the school building, and hey, there was Alisha heading toward her.

But then Alisha stopped dead and stared at her. In a sort of moan, Alisha murmured, "I was so upset I forgot. I didn't call him. God help me."

Jessie wanted to say hi, but her voice came out sounding like Jason's. "Hey, babe. 'Sup?"

Alisha stepped closer, and in a shaky voice she said, "My God, Jessie, go someplace, now. Get away before it's too late."

"What the hell you talking about?"

"You know exactly what I'm talking about."

"Aw, get over yourself."

"Please," Alisha whispered. There she stood, Jessie's best friend, tears in her eyes. Jessie should have felt something.

Great boobs. Look at the boobs on her.

Jason's voice. Right inside Jessie's mind.

Jessie did feel something. Shock. Shame. "No!" she yelled. "Shut up! It's just a game!" Alisha probably thought she was yelling at *her*, which made Jessie feel worse. Turning away, she fled, nearly running, toward the school.

Jason told her, *For God's sake, Sis, chill out. Everything's okay.*

Despite her panic there was calm strength in his presence. Jessie felt soothed the way she had been that night at his grave. She remembered what he had done for her yesterday evening at Dead End Bend, and she lifted her head. She slowed to his oh-so-cool walk. With a proud strut she entered homeroom.

Faces turned to look. Voices faltered to silence. Stark eyes stared. Shane faced her, his handsome face ghost-white.

Jessie greeted him. "Yo, Shane, what was my time?" Going around Dead End Bend last night, she meant.

Shane licked his lips but could not seem to answer.

"Whatever." Jessie sprawled in her desk chair. In the too-long silence, she started to worry again. Hair on her chin. Jason in her head. Jason's hands on her steering wheel. Still half-asleep and numb with fatigue, she felt as if it were all a dream. Had to be. With her head wobbling, she stared at the wall.

A voice blared over the loudspeaker. "Jessica Ressler, report to the office."

She felt the whole classroom full of kids staring at her again as she got up to go.

Whatever they wanted in the office, she didn't care. She had more important things to worry about. They could suspend her or expel her, no problem. She just wanted to go home and go back to bed. Her *own* bed. Start the day over.

"Jessica Ressler," the secretary in the school office told her, "we cannot have you calling yourself Jason on your school papers."

Jessie wanted to ask why not.

Or she wanted to say it didn't matter, because everybody knew she was Jessie.

Really she wanted to say, "Okay, I'll be Jessie from now on. I'm done dressing like my brother." In that moment she suddenly and badly wanted her own pretty clothes back, and her makeup and her Wildflowers in the Rain perfume and her jewelry and her *hair*, which would grow out of the top of her head, not her chin.

But the trouble was, the way the secretary spoke to her— *Jessica Ressler*, that tone of voice—it affected her the way that skinny douche bag of a psychologist had pissed her off. With a new kind of anger. With the quick rage of a rebel.

And when her mouth opened, a deep voice came out. "I *am* Jason," she said.

"Nonsense." But the secretary was staring at her. "Jason died. He is no longer in our files."

But as if she wasn't so sure anymore, the secretary pulled out a drawer and looked through some papers.

Her eyes widened.

She hurried to her computer and typed something on the keyboard.

When she looked at the screen, her mouth opened. At first no sound came out. But then in a voice stretched like a rubber band she called, "Excuse me!" She headed toward the principal's private office in the back.

Jessie heard noise behind her and turned around. In the hallway, on the other side of the office's glass wall, some of Jason's wrestling buddies had gathered. When she looked at them, their faces lit up with grins. God, they were actually glad to see her. Glad. Finally some kids were on her team. It felt great. Jessie grinned back and swaggered out there.

"Hey, dude!"

"Jason! Welcome back!"

"Way to go, man!" One of them punched her hard in the shoulder. She didn't mind. Her muscles were big and strong enough to take it—when had she become so tall, so strong? Jason's Nikes fit her. His jeans fit her.

Or him.

Behind her in the office, the principal's voice was yelling, "I don't care what the system says, the Ressler boy was killed in an accident! We can't all go crazy."

"How'd you do it?" one of Jason's buddies asked.

"Used a girl."

"Cool, man, that's what they're for."

The school counselor stuck his bald head out the office door. "Jessica—"

"Jason."

"*Miss* Ressler, you are excused for the day. Until we get this straightened out. Sign this release slip and go home."

In big, messy handwriting she scrawled *JASON Ressler*. Then she headed for the door.

"You rock, dude!" one of her wrestling buddies called after her.

"*Hi*, Jason," said a girl who was coming in the door as Jessie went out. "I heard you were back!"

"Hi, Jason! Welcome back!" said another girl on the sidewalk outside.

Jessie knew who the girls were, but they had never said hi to her before.

Now look at them smiling.

Jessie smiled back. Jessie walked tall as she strode toward her car.

Alisha was still standing in the parking lot, crying. For a big, strong Black girl she sure looked pitiful, sobbing with her cell phone in her hand. "All I get is a busy signal!" she wailed.

Jessie opened her mouth to talk with Alisha, but Jason's voice came out. "Yo, babe, you wanna go somewhere?"

"Jessie!" Alisha screamed as if somebody were dying. "Try to get away! Try!"

Love those boobs. I'd like to—

Wait a minute. What were girls for? To be used?

No way.

Jessie smoothed her hands across her T-shirt front, checking for her own rosebud breasts. They were gone. All she felt was hard chest. But she couldn't let that bother her too much right now. One thing at a time. Like the facial hair, just another problem to take care of with plastic surgery or whatever, as soon as she went back to being Jessie.

She tried to say something to Alisha in her own voice. It was very, very difficult, like lifting a huge weight, but she did it. "Hey, I'm okay." She could speak only a few words. "This is fun."

Which was true. Being Jason was great. Being a boy was great. Jessie had never in her life felt so bold and strong and not worried about things. She had never felt so *cool*, with kids envying her car, saying hi to her. And Mom smiling, and cooking stuff especially for her—or for Jason—it was like being a hero, that she had been able to do this, to give Jason back to her mother.

"It's horrible," Alisha whispered. "It's sick." Alisha thrust a paper at her, a dirty napkin, actually. "Jessie, please listen. This is your father's phone number. Please call him. Maybe he can help you. I don't know what else to do."

Jessie took the paper napkin, but Jason's voice told Alisha, "What for? I don't need help. See ya." Jessie got into her Z-car and zoomed out of the school parking lot. Not that there was any hurry. She just liked the rush. She took the corner with her tires screaming.

Standing like a wet-eyed zombie, Alisha shuddered, hearing that sound. *The world ought to be screaming,* she thought.

Chapter Fourteen

Jessie's mother was on the phone when Jessie walked into the kitchen.

"Yo, Mudder."

Mom put her hand over the receiver. "It's the school." She smiled a tender, triumphant smile. "You really did it," she whispered. "I knew you would, somehow. At first I just didn't know how. But I knew you'd come back." She uncovered the receiver. "Yes, it has been a very difficult time," she told somebody with quiet dignity. "Please let your records show that I've lost a daughter." She said this as if it made her a little bit sad.

Jessie stood there like she'd been shot. "I'm not dead!" But her voice wouldn't come out loud enough. Her mother did not hear her.

Talking on the phone, Mom lifted her head. "However, I still have my wonderful son."

Then finally it hit Jessie. Mom didn't care what happened to her.

And it wasn't just about her mother.

Jessie didn't have a life anymore.

Like you ever did? mocked Jason's voice inside her head.

Pretend to be Jason? Ha. Forget that. *She* was not being Jason. Jason was being Jason.

In her.

Way more alive than she was, and way stronger. She could feel him taking over, so cool, so selfish—she was no match for his ego.

Yeah, yeah. So what else is new?

But she had not known—she had never dreamed what he was really like. Always before, when they were both alive, she had loved him.

And she had assumed—she had thought—she had hoped he loved her back.

But now she knew the truth. Now she knew how he really felt about her.

Stupid. Clueless. My sister, who thinks she's so smart—such a loser.

Oh, God.

She had been so used.

Standing in the kitchen like a dummy in a store window, Jessie saw her mother hang up the phone and head toward the stairs. Mom wasn't just walking—she was almost dancing.

And Mom was humming a little tune that sounded so happy Jessie couldn't stand it. Panic got her moving. She ran after her mother.

But upstairs, Jessie stopped as if she had been shot again. In her room—Jessie's room—there was Mom taking the stuffed animals off the bed.

"Mom," Jessie called. "Mother."

But her voice came out a whisper, and her mother didn't hear her.

"Mom, it's Jessie. Please. Please, Mom, see me, please talk to me. . . ."

Mom hadn't really spoken to her, Jessie, not one word, since . . .

83

Since who had died?

Mom threw the yellow armadillo and all Jessie's other cuddly babies into a black garbage bag. She stripped the bed and folded the pink plaid comforter, but instead of putting it away, she draped it over one arm, hefted the bag of stuffed animals with the other, carried the things downstairs and dumped them into the big thrift shop box in the closest.

Thrift shop?

Shocked beyond response, Jessie stood petrified in the hallway. She could hear her mother downstairs making a phone call. Then Mom came up again and started scraping Jessie's makeup and jewelry off the dresser into a shoebox.

Including the ruby necklace-and-earrings set Daddy had given her . . .

As if a blood-red button had clicked inside her, letting her move again, Jessie spun around and ran downstairs and out of the house, to the car where she had left the rumpled paper napkin Alisha had given her. With trembling hands she grabbed the cell phone out of her pocket.

W. Richard Ressler, sitting in the insurance office where he worked, shut his cell phone and knew in his stricken heart that all bad times before were nothing compared to this, the worst day of his life.

His ex-wife had just called to inform him that their daughter was dead.

Jessie. Sweet, smart Jessie. Dead.

A tormented sound forced its way out of Rick Ressler's throat, a sound so anguished it seemed barely human, and he laid his head on his desk because he didn't seem to have the strength to sit upright.

He heard startled, anxious co-workers gathering around him, asking what was wrong. He could not answer. Sobbing too hard. His tears soaked the claims forms he had been working on. People died; survivors claimed insurance. It hadn't seemed so wrong up until now.

His ex. Her voice. So cool. The funeral was already over, she said. Jessie was buried.

He should have been furious at her for not notifying him before. But he couldn't react, really, because it was all just impossible. It couldn't be happening. Funeral or no funeral, how could he ever say good-bye to Jessie, oh, beautiful Jessie, oh, his little girl, Jessica?

People were bringing him glasses of water, cold wet paper towels, kneeling beside him and talking about calling a doctor, getting him sedatives. No, thank you. With an effort he raised his head and pressed the towels to his eyes. He blew his nose. He managed to choke out a few words of explanation. Daughter. Dead. Car accident.

His cell phone rang again.

It took most of his remaining strength to reach out and open it. He would not have answered the call except that he saw it came from his old area code, although the phone number itself was unfamiliar.

He put the phone to his ear, mumbled hello. The day felt like a bad dream, so it should have been no surprise that the voice he heard seemed to issue straight out of a nightmare. It said, "Daddy?" but it was the hollow, husky, whispering voice of a specter.

From his own childhood he knew how cruel kids could be. Jason wouldn't do this, but he had a pretty low opinion of some of Jason's friends. His anguish flipped into anger as he barked into the phone, "Who is this?"

"Daddy, it's Jessie." The voice sounded nothing at all like Jessie's. It sounded labored, muffled, some prankster's idea of words forced out from under stone, from the tomb, the crypt. "Help me. Please."

Jessie's father barely heard the last words as he lurched to his feet, exploding, "You goddamn heartless punk, how can you do this? My daughter's dead, and you torment me? Go to hell!" Just snapping the phone shut was not enough. He threw it across the room with such force that it shattered against the wall. Then he collapsed into his chair again, sobbing.

Dad had just told her to go to hell. Mom loved Jason, not her being Jason, not her in any way. Standing beside the Z-car, Jessie wanted to smash it with the cell phone, batter the car and the phone and her miserable self into a pulp. But Jason wouldn't let her. He told her, "Don't try talking anymore," and he put the phone away.

Whose hands were ripping up the paper napkin and tossing the shreds into the gutter? Jessie twisted the passenger-side mirror and looked into it.

Jason's handsome face looked back at her. Jason grinned.

Jessie wanted to curse him and tell him to go to hell, but she could barely speak. "I will get you somehow," she whispered. "I'm not done yet. *I'm not dead.*"

"Shut up. I told you no more talking." Jason's voice grew vicious, and his grin twisted into a sneer. "You're gone, Sis. Your body is in my coffin. They're putting up a grave marker with your name on it. You're nothing. You thought you were somebody? Forget that. You've always been nothing, and you will always be nothing."

Just his saying it made it so true that she could no longer speak aloud. She could only say inside his mind, *I—am—still— Jessie....*

"Not if you know what's good for you. You want to go to wrestling practice, into the locker room? You want to smell the sweat and hear the jokes and have a look around the shower?"

Stop it!

"No, you stop it. Don't kid yourself about what's inside my pants. Which I intend to use. You want to go on dates and see how much you can score? You want to get laid by one of your girlfriends?"

That's sick! You're cruel! You—

"Starting to get a clue, huh? I'm going to do whatever I want to. For starters, I'm going to get my hands on Alisha somehow."

No!

"Hey, if you don't like it, you don't have to know. All you have to do is shut up and go to sleep and stay that way."

If I do that ... Jessie felt terribly tired, more tired than she had ever been in her life, even more tired than she had been getting out of bed this morning. Hazily, as if from a previous existence in another world, she remembered that the third stage of grief was bargaining. *If I go to sleep, will you let Alisha alone? ... Promise? ...*

"Stupid, I don't have to promise anything. Don't bug me anymore or you'll be sorry. Bye-bye."

She flickered, a little campfire going out, no heart left to fight.

Nothingness.

Whistling, Jason walked back to the house, tossing the car keys into the air to hear their happy metallic cry.